A DEADLY WIND BLOWS

AN AL PENNYBACK MYSTERY

CHARLES RAY

NORTH POTOMAC, MD

Printed in the United States of America.

For more information about Uhuru Press books visit our Facebook page at: https://www.facebook.com/UhuruPressbooks

If you've liked this book, consider leaving a review on Amazon.com, Goodreads, or another book review site.

For more information about this author check his author central page on Amazon at: http://www.amazon.com/Charles-Ray/e/B006WMLEZK

Cover photograph and design by the author.

ISBN: 0692325476
ISBN-13: 978-0692325476

Al Pennyback mysteries

Color Me Dead
Memorial to the Dead
Deadline
Dead, White, and Blue
A Good Day to Die
The Day the Music Died
Die, Sinner
Deadly Intentions
Death by Design
Till Death Do Us Part
Deadly Dose
Dead Man's Cove
Dead Men Don't Answer
Deadly Paradise
Kiss of Death
Death in White Satin
Death and Taxis
Deadbeat
A Deadly Wind Blows

Charles Ray

Prologue

I dread thunderstorms. Not some mild phobia mind you, but the teeth chattering kind of fear that makes your legs all rubbery and causes you to want to wet your pants, and leaves you shaking so hard you can hear your bones rattle and you can't breathe. When the wind blows hard, and there's thunder and lightning, I have to fight hard to retain control. I want to run somewhere and hide until it's over. Yeah, it's that kind of fear.

It started in 1960, the summer when I turned 10 years old, and it's all the fault of my cousin, Winston Dodd.

I pretty much learned to control my fear as I grew older, but never completely. Joining the army out of high school helped. In basic training at Fort Polk, an old World War II base in central Louisiana that had been reopened to train soldiers for the war in Vietnam, I had to march through a thunderstorm during basic training, and then later sleep in a hastily-dug fox hole during a torrential downpour that had water up to my hips – which was fortunate because at some point I'd pissed my pants. Later, in Vietnam, I'd had to go on patrols in the jungles of the Central Highlands during thunderstorms that added to the gloom of the already dismal landscape and increased the level of fear we already had of Viet Cong ambushes.

But, back to my cousin, and how I came to fear thunderstorms in the first place.

Winston Dodd was part of the Dodd family, the son of Robert and Stella Dodd. Stella was my father's older sister. Winston was number five of eleven children, all living together on a hundred acre farm on the outskirts of the little town I grew up in. When he was ten, his mother died, and his father, unable to care for eleven children and a farm, decided to farm all but the two oldest boys out to other relatives. Winston was sent to live with our grandmother in a little cottage about a mile from my parent's house. I was an only child, and my grandmother doted on me. I spent almost as much time at her house as I did at my own, and since he was now in effect an only child, we found ourselves spending a lot of time together. Actually, I spent most of my time following him around, and he sort of adopted me as a little brother to replace the three he'd lost when they were all sent to live with various cousins, aunts and uncles, and other assorted relations, mostly in Dallas and Houston.

By the time he turned fifteen, he'd become accustomed to having me around, and for a ten-year-old that was like heaven. We hunted and fished together, went for long walks in the piney woods near my grandmother's cottage, and sometimes just sat in her back yard poring over books from the shelf in her living room, which she called a parlor. Even though I was five years his junior, I could read better than he could – having had to miss a lot of school to help his father on the farm – so, mostly I read and he lay on the grass looking up at the sky.

One Saturday in late July, Winston suggested we go hiking in the big woods behind our house. I had nothing else interesting to do, and I loved spending time with him, so I agreed. We made peanut butter and fried spam sandwiches and filled two thermos bottles with lemonade, which we put in the little green knapsacks we'd made from an old tent that was too ragged to use anymore. We found the instructions for making knapsacks in one of my grandmother's books.

We set out around ten in the morning. The sun was high, and so was the humidity, but we'd grown up with these conditions, and didn't mind, even though our shirts were soaked with sweat by the time we made the deep shade of

3

the piney forest. Not that it was any cooler under the trees, but it meant we didn't have the merciless sun beating down on us.

The trees towered over us, great conical structures soaring up forty to a hundred feet. We could see the slate blue sky in the spaces between the tops of the trees. The floor of the forest was covered with dead and dying leaves and pine needles, creating a soft, spongy carpet that absorbed the sound of our footsteps. In fact, the only sound was the soft murmuring of an occasional stray breeze and the whispering of pine needles and leaves rubbing together high above us.

We headed southeast toward the big swamp that bisected the forest, a large tract of woods, with pine, hickory, oak and wild plum trees. Many of the trees were covered with ivy vines, with only the larger branches able to break through to get sunlight. Winston said he'd heard it was a great place to see big bullfrogs. There was this place in town where a lot of the old white people ate that served frogs legs. They paid a dollar a frog if you brought in fresh caught ones. We were hoping to gig six or seven big ones. With that much money, we could keep ourselves stocked up with Royal Crown cola and graham crackers for a month.

We reached the edge of the swamp just before noon. Here the pines were replaced by gnarled cypress trees whose limbs were festooned with gray moss that dripped down to the dirty green water below. There weren't many cypress trees, though, so the broad swamp stretching before us was brightly lit by the sun, which was by now beating down from straight overhead. The water was dirty green, like the moss on the trees.

The ground at the edge of the swamp was muddy and even softer than that in the forest, and we took care where we put our feet. There were places you could sink in up to your knees, or even deeper. Thinking about getting caught in that muck wasn't a pleasant feeling.

We found a dry hummock a few yards upslope from the edge of the swamp and put our knapsacks down. With the croaking of frogs off in the distance as a musical accompaniment, we took out our lunches – soggy peanut butter, jelly, and spam sandwiches – which we washed down with warm RC Colas. After we'd finished eating, we went back to the edge of the scummy brown water and began our search for frogs. Our gigs were a couple of broken broom handles with bent nails in the ends, and we'd brought along an old croaker sack which we'd hope to fill with our catch.

Had we not been so intent upon locating the frogs whose loud croaking indicated that they were near, we might have noticed the change in the weather.

The first sign of change we missed was a slight cooling in the breeze blowing across the water. That was followed by a darkening of the sky as clouds began to form to the south and, pushed by the wind, roll our way.

What *did* finally get our attention was the silence. As if someone had flipped a switch, the croaking stopped. The heavy silence was like having a blanket draped over my head. Winston was standing to the side and just in front of me, peering into the dark water. He looked at me, and then up at the sky. A worried look caused his light brown brow to crease.

"Looks like it's 'bout to rain," he said.

I looked up. The bright blue sky had turned dark gray. The sharp smell of ozone joined the musty smell of the swamp water.

"You think we oughta head for home?" I asked. "Mama won't like it if we get soaked and track water in the house."

He put his gig in the sack and held it out to me to put mine in.

"Yeah," he said. "If we hurry, maybe we'll make it before the rain starts."

Tying off the neck of the croaker sack, he tied it to his knapsack which he tossed over his shoulder. I grabbed my own sack and followed him as he headed at a fast pace back the way we'd come. By the time we were back in the woods, the sky was a dark gray. It was like early evening.

What Winston hadn't said, but what I knew, was that it wasn't getting wet that bothered him. We'd played in the rain many times. We both knew that the sudden change, especially the frogs getting so silent, meant only one thing – a real bad storm was brewing. You don't want to get caught outside in a storm in East Texas. There's usually lots of lightning, the wind is flinging all manner of dangerous stuff around like confetti, hail stones the size of baseballs come plummeting out of the sky, and now and then a big black tornado springs up out of nowhere, ripping barns and houses apart like so much kindling. In other words, storms in this part of the country can kill you if you get caught outside.

The sudden boom of a thunder clap caused us both to jump. He increased his pace, causing me to almost have to run to keep up with him. I could feel a spreading warmth down the inside of my left leg. I'd peed myself.

Summer thunderstorms come on suddenly in East Texas. One minute the sky is bright blue and the heat is sucking the sweat from every pore in your body. The next, the air is chilly and the wind is whipping across your skin and blowing bits of trash into your face. The bad part, though, is when the thunder starts coming in rolling waves, sounding like dynamite or big guns going off, and you can feel the vibrations in the air and through your feet as the ground seems to shake.

In the deep woods we couldn't see the lightning, but I knew sharp spears of electricity were lancing from the sky toward the ground. You don't want to be outside when the weather turns nasty like that. If you're in the open, you can become a rod, attracting a bolt of lightning, and if you're around big trees that act like natural lightning rods, you can get really messed up if you're near one that gets hit by lightning. I'd once seen an old cow that had been struck by lightning. The fur was singed, except for where the bolt had struck – that was burned clean away – and the smell of burned flesh could be detected nearly a quarter mile away.

We were fair running now. Ducking right and left as we made our way through the trees, trying to stay on the trail as much as possible and not trip over a fallen branch, or step in a bog. Behind us I could hear the hissing of rain and the roar of the wind as it whipped the smaller limbs off the trees. That was another thing that scared me. Some of the limbs that broke off flew through the air like little spears. A high wind could drive one right through you.

Along with the warm liquid that had completely wet the front of my pants, there were hot, salty tears flowing down both cheeks. I just knew the two of us were going to die out there. The woods were big and deep. Our bodies could be out there for days before anyone found us. The buzzards would likely find us first and after a few days there'd be nothing left but bleached bones.

"We're not gonna make it," Winston said. "We need to find a place to hole up until the lightning and rain passes."

He slowed down, causing me to crash into his back and send him sprawling face down on the wet floor of the woods. For a moment the both of us just lay there breathing heavily, and then he pushed me off and stood, brushing the wet leaves and clumps of mud from his shirt, trousers and face. I looked around. The ground rose on our right, and through the trees I spotted what looked like a small cave where the ground rose straight up into a six foot tall hill. I pointed.

"Maybe we can fit in there," I said loudly, but with a hopeful note.

Winston looked around. A stream that flowed into the swamp was off to the left, and the area immediately adjacent to the dark opening was free of tall trees, so we probably wouldn't get caught in a flash flood or hit by a bolt of lightning.

He screwed his face in concentration. Just then

the sky opened up and it started raining. The wind was blowing so hard the drops of rain hit the side of our faces like little pebbles. The thunder was so loud it was hard to hear myself talk. The clearing we were in lit up as bright as day from lightning that seemed just overhead. The smell of ozone was stronger.

The lightning strike helped Winston make up his mind. He grabbed my hand and started running toward the hill. I had to pump hard to keep from being dragged.

The hole in the hill was just that. It went in about four feet – hardly a cave – but thanks to the direction the wind was blowing little of the rain penetrated all the way back. We huddled against the black earth wall, holding onto each other, trembling and jerking with each crash of thunder or flash of lightning.

I was so relieved at being out of the storm it took me a few minutes to realize that there might be scorpions or spiders in this hole in the ground – or even snakes. My whole body started shaking at the thought – I'd come close to being killed by a thunderstorm, only to end up being stung or bitten by some poisonous creature, and being in a hole in the ground, our bodies might *never* be found.

I tried not to cry, but I couldn't help it. Winston pulled me in close and tried to reassure me, but his own voice was quavering, so I knew he was as scared as I was. Strangely, that helped make me feel better, and I soon stopped crying. But, I didn't stop shaking.

The thunderstorm passed in thirty minutes, but it seemed like a lifetime. With a final crash of thunder and several neon flashes of lightning, the rain stopped and the area outside our hole in the hill turned from dark gray and green to a bright emerald color. The birds and insects started chirruping as if nothing had happened.

I was fortunate we'd been caught in the rain and soaked, because I'd been so scared that we'd be fried by lightning or swept away by a torrent of water I'd peed myself, and the rain masked my little accident. Winston had kept quiet, playing the strong one, but from the way his body trembled, I knew he'd been as frightened as me.

We didn't speak as we walked home. With the rain gone, the heat came back, so our clothes were only damp when we got back to our grandma's house – about what they would have been from sweat if it hadn't rained.

Winston and I never spoke of that day in the woods – not to each other or to anyone else. But, from that hot day in July when I was ten years old, whenever I hear thunder I get this cold feeling in my chest and find it hard to breathe.

Charles Ray

1.

"Al, how'd you like to spend some time on the beach?"

Quincy Chang, a partner at Holcombe, Stein and Chang, the law firm that has me on a ten thousand buck a month retainer, and one of my oldest friends, smiled broadly at me across his wide wooden desk as he played with a buff colored folder. He didn't fool me, though. I knew there had to be a catch to his offer of an all-expense paid trip.

"Depends on where the beach is," I said. "Last time we went to paradise, we almost got killed, remember?"

That had been a trip to Hawaii to attend the wedding of one of his relatives. A sniper had almost spoiled the trip by trying to kill the groom. That had not been a fun trip. The way he winced I knew he remembered.

"No problems," he said. "This one's close, and no snipers – at least, there shouldn't be."

I wasn't in the mood to say no. There were a number of reasons for that. There was the ten thousand a month Quince's firm paid me for one thing. I'd also been promising Sandra that we'd take a vacation, and if I was getting paid expenses to boot, it shouldn't be that much of a problem. In return for the generous retainer, I did scut work for the firm; chasing down deadbeats who refused to pay their bills, and occasionally running down someone to get a legal paper signed. There was also the fact that Quincy Chang was one of my oldest and closest friends.

"Where's the beach, and what do I have to do in return for this vacation?"

He opened the folder and removed an eight by ten glossy photograph which he slid across the desk toward me.

"I need you to find this woman," he said. "And, convince her to come back to DC."

The photo was a black and white studio portrait of a woman who looked to be in her mid-forties. From the tones, her close cropped hair looked medium brown. She had light colored eyes that stared defiantly at the camera over a nose that was a bit too large for her oval face.

"What's her story?"

He removed another paper, a long legal document with seals and signatures and a lot of mumbo jumbo written in the legalese that lawyers seem to prefer over plain English.

"This is Megan Sutliff," he said. "She's one of two heirs to Sutliff Pharmaceuticals. The other is her twin brother, Melvin. Her mother died when they were teenagers, and her father, Conrad Sutliff, just died recently. She and her brother jointly inherited the estate, and we need her here for the reading and probate of his will."

"Why not just give her a call, or send a telegram?"

"We don't have a contact number or address for her. She's been incommunicado for the past ten years, when she cleaned out the trust fund her father had set up for her and left town. Her last known address was just a town – Manteo, North Carolina. It's on the Outer Banks. We contacted the town sheriff, but his office had no record of her."

Which is why they have me on retainer. When the Post Office or local law enforcement can't find a person, the firm sends me to act the ferret. I don't have to worry about warrants or privacy laws. But, I usually have a little more current information about the prey – ten years is a long time and a trail can grow awful cold in that time.

"How do you know she hasn't moved somewhere else, to another state even? This could be a wild goose chase," I said.

"We can't be sure." He shrugged and played with the legal document, making snapping sounds as he bent and straightened it. "But, it's at least a place to start. I figure you'll be able to pick up her trail if it exists. If it turns out to be a bust, you'll at least have had a nice time on the beach on the firm."

I'd taken my late wife Sarah and our son Ethan to the Outer Banks when I was stationed at Ft. Bragg, a big army base in central North Carolina. We'd all enjoyed the crystal white sand and the cool breezes blowing in from the Atlantic. In addition, I'd gotten a kick out of visiting Kitty Hawk, where the Wright brothers had done their test flights. I was pretty sure Sandra would like it as well.

"Okay, I'll take the job," I said. "How long should I look for her before I give up?"

"Hell, Al, you're the detective. I'll leave that up to you."

Of course he could, and would. I wouldn't take a day longer than necessary – he knew that – but, I'd also give it my best shot. If Megan Sutliff was to be found, I had as good a chance as any of finding her. If, on the other hand, she really, really didn't *want* to be found, it might be a challenge even for me.

"Deal," I said. "Now, tell me everything you know about her."

Some of what Quince told me came from the rest of the papers in the folder, the rest from what he knew of the Sutliff family from having been the attorney of record for Conrad Sutliff for more than ten years. As lawyers have a tendency to do, he told me much more than I really needed to know. I imagine some of what he told me might even be protected by attorney-client privilege, but, as an employee of the law firm I think I was exempt. He also knew, though, that I wouldn't divulge sensitive information.

Conrad Sutliff had inherited Sutliff Pharmaceuticals from his father Morgan at the age of twenty-five when the elder Sutliff died of a massive heart attack. Through a combination of hard work and hard ball tactics, Conrad had turned a small pill manufacturing concern into one of the biggest purveyors of medications on the east coast, ranking in the top ten of the industry by the time of his own death – also from a heart attack.

Megan Sutliff and her twin brother Melvin were the only children, and the last of their line. They were forty-six and neither had ever married. It pleased me that I'd been pretty close in the estimate of her age from the photo in the file.

Ten years ago, Megan had left the DC area after a family squabble, the details of which Quince didn't know, and except for the occasional Christmas card, postmarked from Manteo, North Carolina, with no specific return address, hadn't had any contact with her father or brother. The Christmas cards had stopped more than five years ago. Melvin Sutliff had worked with his father in the company, and after the elder Sutliff's suffered his first heart attack a year earlier had taken over running it.

As Quince spoke, I made a mental note that Megan hadn't bothered returning home even after her father became ill, nor had she returned for his funeral. This could have been due to the inability to contact her.

Quince said Melvin had sent her several letters, addressed 'General Delivery,' but they'd all been returned as 'undeliverable.' It struck me as strange that Melvin hadn't gone to North Carolina to try and find his sister, and I mentioned this to Quince.

"I don't know what went on between them," Quince said. "But, it's clear that there's no love lost between the two of them. Frankly, I think Melvin would be just as happy if you didn't find her. Unfortunately, the will names her as an equal inheritor, and her presence is essential for probate."

"I imagine probate is a lengthy process," I said. "How much time are we talking here?"

"In complicated cases, especially those without a proper last will and testament, it can take years. Fortunately, Conrad Sutliff's will is in order," he said. Our firm was named as executor, and as his personal attorney, I'm the personal representative. Under DC Code, section 20-704(b), I'm required to contact each heir – Megan and Melvin in this case – to provide them with the details of the disposition of Conrad's property and assets. In addition, I have to settle his outstanding debts and obligations, which are sizeable, and then ensure that the heirs get equal shares of the balance. Even with the debts paid, the two of them will split eight hundred million dollars, including bank accounts and property, the largest being Sutliff Pharmaceuticals. I've begun the process of filing documents with the probate court, but I need to get Megan to either accept the terms of the will or renounce her inheritance. Failing that, Melvin could file for the court to determine disposition."

"Has he expressed any concerns about the terms of the will?"

"Not specifically, but he has pressed me to move the process along as quickly as possible. He says he has plans for expanding the company, and they've had to be put on hold until Conrad's will is finally probated."

I reached across the desk and picked up the photograph.

"Mind if I take this? When was it taken, by the way?"

"I'm not sure, but it was before she left home. I think she would have been in her early thirties at the time."

Shit, I thought, I'd been way off about her age. If she looked like forty when she was thirty, there was no telling what she looked like now. This might not be so easy after all. I sighed and shrugged. Quince smiled. Damn him. He knew what I was thinking – what I'd been thinking – and seemed to be enjoying my discomfiture. If he hadn't one of my best friends, I would have made a smart ass remark. But, it wasn't his fault, so I kept my trap shut. To his credit, he did take another buff folder from his desk so I wouldn't have to damage the picture by folding it and putting it in my pocket.

I looked at my watch. It was getting on to noon, which I'd figured anyway because my stomach was making little bubbling noises.

"Too late to get started today," I said. "I need to get Sandra packed, and that'll take a few hours. It's a six or seven hour drive to the Outer Banks, depending on the traffic on I-95, so I guess we'll hit the road in the morning. Tomorrow's Saturday, so if we get going early enough we might miss the weekend traffic."

"No problem. Keep good records of your expenses," he said. "Sandra's too. This trip's on the firm. We'll cover expenses for both of you – anything other than furs or jewels."

I could live with that. Sandra and I hadn't had a vacation in a while, and having one paid for by someone else would be a treat for the both of us – despite my probably having to spend most of it driving up and down back roads and bugging people for information about a woman who apparently didn't want to be found. But, that's what I do.

The hunt was on.

2.

I've been a private detective for over a decade.

Quincy, who I often call Quince, which he doesn't particularly like, and my other best friend, Buster Mayweather, a Metropolitan DC police detective, talked me into getting my license and working as a PI when I retired from the army after my wife and son were killed in an auto accident. Along with the retainer from Quince's firm, my assistant Heather Bunche and I make do with the odd over-the-transom case – and believe me, some of them are *odd*. A.E. Pennyback, Confidential Inquiries – I'm Albert Einstein Pennyback, thus the name of the company – does well enough. Our bills get paid, Heather gets a nice bonus now and then, and we have a nice cash reserve for emergencies. Oh, and by the way, no one – and I mean *no one* – calls me Albert, or Albert Einstein. I'm just Al to my friends, and Mr. Pennyback to those who've just met me. I got the moniker courtesy of my mother who was enamored of the German scientist, and had hopes that I'd grow up to be just like him – I disappointed her by joining the army right out of high school. Growing up in East Texas where calling people by their first and middle name was the custom, I went through the first five years of school taking jibes from the kids in school. I got my growth spurt just before my sixth year, learned how to use my fists, and after that I was just Al to everyone who knew better, and that crazy bastard who'll crack your skull to the ones who didn't.

My own expenses are minimal. I own a small non-working farm near Potomac, Maryland, just off River Road, where I currently live with Sandra Winter, a teacher at Calvert High School in the District. Sandra and I met during one of those odd over-the-transom cases; hit it off after a rocky start, and by mutual consent entered into a monogamous relationship. At forty, she's ten years my junior, but I'm pretty fit for my age, so she has no complaints.

We run through the forest behind the farm house almost every morning, after which we work out on a heavy bag I have hanging in the barn. That works up quite a sweat and keeps us both in shape. I've been teaching her a little taekwondo, the Korean martial art I learned in the army, and she's taken to it like a frog to flies. After our workout, she showers while I meditate, then cooks breakfast while I shower. We eat together, clean the kitchen, then she goes off to school and I go off to do my detecting. Sometimes I cook, and on weekends we often do it together.

After leaving Quince's office, I dropped by a Burger King on K Street and had a quick burger, fries and coke for lunch, and then went back to the office to brief Heather on the case. I figured I'd be gone at least a week, but she recently got her own PI license, so she could handle anything from Quince's firm, and just put off the walk-ins until I got back.

The office taken care of, I jumped into my green Volkswagen that Sandra bought me for my fiftieth birthday and headed home. I left the office at four, so I managed to beat most of the Friday commuter traffic, except for the smart ones who knock off early to get a jump on the weekend.

Having beat Sandra home – she'd planned to do shopping at one of the malls on Rockville Pike after her last summer school class for the day at Carter High School in the District's Southeast area - I took a quick shower, changed into a tee shirt and brown chinos, and prepared supper. Breaded pork chops, corn on the cob, fried okra, a salad made of fresh spinach, onions, sweet peppers, and tomatoes, and fluffy cornbread sticks containing sweet corn and jalapeno peppers – cooked like I remember my grandmother doing when I was a kid. I topped that off with a pitcher of unsweetened iced tea, and put a bottle of white wine in the fridge so that by the time Sandra got home from the summer school she'd been supervising it would be just cold enough. For my own enjoyment, I put aside two bottles of *Corona* beer. I can do white wine in a pinch, but if I have to drink wine, I prefer a nice dry red, which I'm told doesn't go well with pork.

I was just flipping the cornbread from the skillet onto a platter when I heard the *tick-tick* of Sandra's heels on the tile floor of the kitchen. She came up behind me and put her arms around my waist, pressing her breasts against my shoulder blades. I'm six-one, and she's nearly six feet, so she can do that without having to tiptoe.

"Hm, the food smells great, and so do you," she murmured into my ear. "Don't know which I want to eat first."

I put the platter of bread on the counter and rotated until her firm breasts were pushed against my chest. I put my arms around her and with my hands on her lower back, pulled her close.

"You smell pretty good, yourself," I said. "But, the burger I had for lunch was digested hours ago, so we do food first."

"Oh, you're no fun," she said. "Okay, let me go shower and change into something more comfortable."

She kissed me lightly on the cheek and after extricating herself from my embrace turned and walked out of the kitchen. The sway of her hips as she walked told me what she thought of my food first idea.

The sight of her walking away, which is almost as titillating as the sight of her walking toward me, almost made me change my mind. The smell of freshly fried breaded pork chops, though, yanked me back to the reality that I a growling stomach could spoil a romantic mood, so I began setting the table.

As we were finishing our meal, and having a second drink; her white wine, me beer; I told her about Quince's offer.

"A few days at the beach," she said. "Just what I need. Today was the last day of summer school, and a few days lolling in the sand will help me get ready for the start of the new school year in two months."

I felt good about not hassling Quince about the assignment. Sandra had spent all of June and the first week of July conducting reading and writing classes for the students who hadn't been able to score high enough on their final exams to pass to the next grade. Bad enough that she had to deal with them nine months out of the year – having to give up part of her summer was above and beyond the call of duty, even for a teacher as dedicated as she was. I owed her a trip, and more.

"I'm not sure how much time I'll be able to spend on the beach with you," I said. "I do have to earn my pay."

She smiled coyly at me over the rim of her wine glass.

"That's okay, babe. As long as you spend your evenings with me, I can live with that."

"Speaking of evenings," I said. "Are you ready for dessert?"

Charles Ray

3.

We arose bright and early Saturday morning. The sun was just peeking over the tops of the trees to the east when we did an abbreviated morning run, ten minutes on the heavy bag, showered, and ate a light breakfast.

I wasn't sure what to pack for the trip. Not being a suit and tie kind of person, I only have a couple of outfits appropriate for a venue requiring coat and tie. More often than not, I wear khakis or chinos with a plain brown or blue shirt, plain black shoes similar to those I wore for twenty years in the army, and a light jacket if there's a nip in the air. I hadn't been back to North Carolina since leaving Fort Bragg, but I recalled that outside the main cities of Raleigh and Charlotte, few people went in for coat and tie, so I threw several pairs of jeans and heavy duty pants, along with a good number of long sleeved shirts – mostly blue and brown – into my beat up old travel bag. I then stuffed a week's worth of underwear and socks into the sides and closed it. I was ready to go.

Sandra had watched me pack, occasionally smiling and shaking her head. She'd put two medium sized suitcases on the bed and was neatly folding pants, skirts, blouses, underwear, swim suit, and the like, and then carefully stacking each item so that when she was finished, her two bags looked like they were ready to be filmed for one of those upscale travel or hotel ads.

"You forgot to pack a swim suit," she said as I hefted my bag.

I dropped the bag on the floor and rummaged through the dresser until I found my old blue swim trunks. Balling them up, I crammed them in next to my socks and reclosed my bag. Sandra made a sniffing noise. I ignored her.

We'd decided to take the Volkswagen because it got better gas mileage than Sandra's car. Her two suitcases took up the trunk, so my bag went on the back seat.

After a thorough check of the house to make sure the stove was off, no faucets were dripping, and the doors were all secure, we were ready to go.

At half past seven, we turned east onto River Road, and headed for the I-495 beltway. Traffic was light on River Road, and on the Beltway until we got around to the Tysons Corner area, where it was stop and go to I-95. Northbound traffic on I-95 was heavy, but not much was heading south, so we were able to make up some of the time lost on I-495, until we began hitting backed up traffic near Woodbridge, so I took the exit ramp to U.S. Route 1 south to Fredericksburg, arriving at the outskirts of the city at 10:00.

My plan was to take I-95 south, and then take the I-295 bypass just north of Richmond to I-64 east toward Norfolk. Quince had suggested I get on U.S Route 17, just south of Fredericksburg, and take that less-traveled route, which would link up with I-64 near Newport News, Virginia. From there, he'd said, it was a relatively short two-hour drive to the North Carolina state line, and except for summer vacationers, a smooth drive to our final destination. I stayed on Route 1 through Fredericksburg, and took the left onto 17 just south of the city.

The scenery along Route 1 – tacky motels, auto repair shops, rundown strip malls, one-story houses in need of paint jobs – quickly changed when we were only a little ways east of Fredericksburg on 17. There were still the strip malls perched alongside the road, their gravel parking lots filled with pickups and rusty sedans, machine shops – though most also repaired tractors – and small houses set back from the road – often with a rusty old auto on blocks in the front yard. But, this was truly rural country; with stately old farm houses set on hills overlooking neatly tended fields of corn and other crops; roadside stands selling fruits and vegetables; small towns that sat astride the highway, often with gun shops, bait shops, and mom and pop diners.

At the town of Tappahannock, where Routes 17 and 360 intersect, the highway runs along the Rappahannock River, glimpses of which can be seen through the trees that line the road. As you near Newport News, an industrial port city at the confluence of the Rappahannock and James Rivers, you begin to see fewer farm houses, and more mansions surrounded by manicured lawns rather than farm fields – one of the places Virginia's rich go to get away from the hoi polloi – and, gated communities guarded by video surveillance systems and rent-a-cops patrolling in golf carts.

The area of Virginia known as the Tidewater is awash with rivers. The waters of the Rappahannock and James Rivers are joined by the York River before flowing into Chesapeake Bay and subsequently into the Atlantic Ocean.

We stopped at Gloucester Point, just north of the bridge that spanned the York River, to top of the Volkswagen's tank, use the toilets, and grab a quick bite from the little convenience store attached to the gas station. After crossing the bridge, we drove through the Colonial National Historical Park, little of which can be seen from the highway. We promised ourselves we'd tour the park on our way back through.

We could have stayed on Route 17 into North Carolina, but both of us had seen enough of the countryside, so when we came to I-64, we took the on ramp and headed toward Hampton. The signs on I-64 gave us two choices to get to North Carolina's Outer Banks; stay on the interstate and loop around east of Norfolk, or take the I-664 loop to the west of Norfolk to hook up with Route 17 south again. Sandra had purchased a map when we stopped for gas, and had it open on her lap. She assured me that the latter route seemed shorter and seemed to go through more scenic country, so I took the ramp to I-664, which ran past the Newport News marine terminal, crossing the James River via a combination bridge/tunnel, and zipped past the town of Suffolk and Chesapeake. A sign at State Road 168 indicated the exit toward the Outer Banks.

From the exit, after paying a toll, we were soon in North Carolina. More small towns, roadside fruit stands, and small cafes, along with signs advertising the sights and activities of the Outer Banks. Ten miles after crossing the state line, we had a great view of the Intercoastal Waterway on our left. There were a few stately homes with ocean views, but far more modest houses surrounded by fields of corn, cabbage, or fruit trees. At the town of Barco, North Carolina, Route 168 became 158. According to Sandra's map, we could stay on that highway, with the Intercoastal Waterway to our right and the Atlantic to our left, to the town of Whalebone, where we could turn east on U.S. Route 64, cross the waterway to Roanoke Island, and then go north to Manteo.

It was a pleasant drive, despite having to watch out for college students enjoying the last days of summer, activities that involved lots of alcohol and borderline dangerous behavior.

We arrived in Manteo at 4:20 in the afternoon.

I hadn't been expecting much, but the place surprised me. A small town located near the northern end of Roanoke Island, it was tidy, and lacking the usual proliferation of chain motels I'd expected in a resort town. There were a number of tourists strolling along the main east-west streets, distinguished from the locals by the trendy shorts, Hawaiian shirts and flip-flop sandals, most with cameras hung around their necks. We drove around a while until we found a suitable looking bed and breakfast inn on Fernando Street, not far from the waterfront. I pulled into the gravel parking lot off to the side. There weren't any other cars in the Dew Drop Inn lot, which didn't mean anything, since at this time of day most of the visitors would be out sightseeing. Sandra stayed in the car while I went into the small reception area to check for vacancies.

A young woman with flame red hair piled high on her head, dark purple eye shadow highlighting her bright blue eyes, and tiny breasts poking against a pink blouse, stood behind the counter. She smiled brightly as I approached.

"Hi. Y'all looking for a room?"

"If you have any vacancies, I'd like a double for about a week," I said.

"Y'all are in luck," she said. "We got a nice room overlooking the water. If you're renting for the whole week, it'll be a hundred dollars a night – one twenty-five if you're renting by the day."

It was bit more than I'd expected for such a small town, but it *was* a resort town, and this was the high season. The firm was paying for it, so it would have to do. I took out my credit card and driver's license and put them on the counter.

"Okay, one room for two people for the whole week," I said.

"It'll be ten dollars a day extra for the extra person," she said, looking at me with a questioning look, as if she expected me to say no.

"That's fine. Do you have a restaurant here?"

"No, but we do serve breakfast in the lounge." She pointed to a small room off to the side with a large credenza and eight tables, each with four chairs. "If you like seafood, there's a pretty good café just down the street on the water."

I nodded my assent, and she slid a registration card across for me to fill out. While I filled in the required information, I watched her out of the corner of my eye. Her smile never wavered, but I could tell she was giving me a good eyeballing. I decided I might as well get started looking for Megan Sutliff, and this was as good a place as any. I took my PI card out and put it on the counter.

"I'm here on a combination business-pleasure trip," I said. She picked the card up and studied it carefully. "I work for a law firm in DC, and they've sent me here to try and find a person who is reportedly living here in Manteo. Maybe you've seen her around. Her name is Megan Sutliff."

"I've been living here my whole life, and I've never heard of anyone named Sutliff. How long's she supposed to have been here?"

"About ten years, I think."

She shook her head, causing the curls on top to bounce.

"Nope, ain't nobody here by that name. We only got about fifteen hundred people living here full time, so I'd know if there was."

I hadn't expected to strike pay dirt on the first try, but it hit hard that a native had never even heard the name. Then, I had a thought – maybe Sutliff was using an assumed name. It made sense if she really wanted to cut herself off from her family.

"I have a photo of her in my car," I said. "It's an old one, but I'm told it still resembles her. You mind taking a look at it?"

She nodded. While she got my registration ready, I went back out and took the folder from the back seat where I'd put it. Back inside, I took the photo out and put it on the counter. She looked at it for a long time, and then shook her head.

"I've never seen this woman before," she said.

She sounded pretty certain. I couldn't let that floor me, though. She was just one person. I'd give it another few tries. Megan Sutliff had been in Manteo – I didn't doubt the validity of Quince's information. She might have departed, but if she'd been in a town this small, *someone* would have seen her. I'd just have to turn over a few more rocks to get a lead on her whereabouts.

Charles Ray

4.

Sandra and I checked into our room. It wasn't large, but it was comfortable, and it did have a fantastic view of the waterway and the beach.

Opposite the door there was a queen-sized canopied bed with a flower print blue spread and two pillows with dark blue coverings. A mahogany nightstand upon which sat a small lamp with a filigreed shade was on one side and the window with the water view on the other. Pink lace curtains on the window were tied back, giving a triangular view of the dark blue Intercoastal Waterway and the light blue sky with wisps of clouds floating lazily by. Two cane chairs sat in the corner to the left and a small round coffee table, made of the same cane material, sat between them. To the right was a mahogany armoire that almost reached the ceiling. With three drawers at the bottom and a double-door top, it was the only storage space, but sufficient for what we'd packed. Our shoes made clicking sounds on the polished wood floor as we entered. There was no telephone and no TV, so there'd be no interruptions, and we would have to come up with our own entertainment.

"A quaint little place," Sandra said as she put her bags on the foot of the bed and began unpacking.

"I don't think we'll be spending too many of our daylight hours in the room," I said. "From here the beach looks quite inviting, and I do have some investigating to do."

She smiled coyly as she folded each item of clothing before stacking it neatly in the top drawer of the armoire.

"True I suppose, and we shouldn't need any distractions at night. So, what do you want to do first?"

"I thought maybe we'd just walk around and get to know the town. Maybe a stroll along the beach until supper?"

"Sounds like a great idea," she said. "Just let me change."

She stripped and pulled a pair of brown, mid-thigh shorts and a beige scoop-neck blouse from the drawer and put them on. She then slipped her feet into a pair of dark brown sandals. I was wearing the same thing I'd driven in, my chinos and a long sleeve blue shirt, and I didn't feel like changing. I did, though, remember to take the folder with Megan Sutliff's photo.

Arm in arm we left the inn and headed down the sidewalk in the direction of the waterfront and beach.

The sun was getting low and the shadows longer, with much of the sidewalk shaded by the two and three-story buildings. It wasn't what I'd call crowded, but there were a number of people, strolling and going in and out of the shops along the street. We attracted not a few glances – appreciative looks at Sandra from the men, and inquisitive looks at me by some of the women. I detected a few frowns, whether from jealousy from the fact that I was in the company of the most beautiful woman on the street, or that we were in this town something of a mismatched pair – me tall and medium brown, with close-cropped, slightly curly hair, and her tall and blonde, with skin lightly bronzed from sunning on the back porch of the farm house – I really couldn't say, and as long as it was just looks and not something more direct, I really didn't give a damn. Sandra seemed not to notice. She was accustomed to men ogling her and women looking envious, and paid it no attention.

As we neared the beach and waterfront, I noticed a small grocery store; a Pik and Pay, on the corner next to a souvenir shop.

"Let's check out the local produce," I said.

Sandra frowned at me.

"You're not seriously thinking about buying something and lugging it on the beach, are you?"

"No." I laughed. "But, I figure if anyone in this town knows who lives here, it'll be a local merchant. Everyone has to buy groceries at some point. I thought I'd show Sutliff's photo and see if anyone has ever seen her."

"Okay, as long as it doesn't take too long," she said. "I'd really like to get in a walk on the beach before sunset."

"I promise it'll be a quick in and out."

A bell over the door rang loudly as we entered. The place was small, with narrow aisles between the well-stocked shelves. The milk coolers and meat counter ran along the back wall. The lone clerk, a paunchy middle aged man with a stained apron around his ample waist, stood behind a counter at the right, looking through the window at the passersby. There was one other customer, a tall, gaunt woman wearing overalls and a plaid shirt. Her long blonde hair fell to her shoulders from beneath a wide-brimmed straw hat. She wore dark sunglasses perched halfway down her prominent nose. She glanced at us briefly as we entered and turned toward the clerk, who smiled broadly as we approached.

"Something I can do for you folks?" he asked.

I took the photo from the folder and laid it on the counter. Taking out my PI ID, I laid it next to the photo.

"I'm a private investigator," I said. "I'm looking for this woman on behalf of a law firm in Washington, DC."

When he realized we weren't in the store to buy anything, he frowned, but his curiosity got the better of him.

"A real live PI! Like Magnum?"

"Yes, a real live PI," I said. "But, not like Magnum. I mostly do jobs like this – looking for people for my employers. Have you ever seen her?"

He picked the photo up and held it at arms-length, squinting at it.

"Can't say I've ever seen her," he said, handing the photo back to me. "She supposed to live in these parts?"

"She's originally from the Washington area, but she moved down here about ten years ago."

"Is that there a current picture? Folks can change a lot in ten years."

"No, it's ten years old, but I'm told she hasn't changed all that much."

The woman had finished her shopping and was approaching the counter with a basket laden with cans and boxes. She put it on the end of the counter.

"Be with you in a minute, Miz Savage," the clerk said. He turned his attention back to me. "Sorry I can't help you Mr. . . ." He looked down at my ID. "Mr. Pennyback. I don't recall ever seeing anybody looks like this. What's her name?"

"Megan Sutliff," I said.

The waiting woman made a rasping sound in her throat. The clerk reached for her basket and started removing the items.

"Sorry for keeping you waiting, Miz Savage. That name don't really ring a bell to me, and I know most everyone lives in and around this town. Miz Savage, you ever heard of a woman named Megan Sutliff living in Manteo?"

"No," she said in a quiet, husky voice. "There's no one around here with that name."

She didn't look at him when she answered, nor did she look at me or Sandra. She kept her eyes fixed on her basket of goods.

I held the photo up. "Have you ever seen this woman?"

"No," she said, barely glancing at it.

So much for southern hospitality, I thought.

"Well, thank you both for your time," I said.

I retrieved my ID, and after placing the photo back in the folder, turned to leave. When we were outside, Sandra nudged me with her shoulder.

"Can we go to the beach now?"

I shrugged.

"Might as well."

When we reached the last north-south cross street before the beach, a black BMW turned the corner, causing us to step quickly back onto the sidewalk. I only got a glimpse of the driver, but I recognized the blonde from the grocery store. She drove looking straight ahead, her hands gripped tightly on the wheel.

"Wow," Sandra said, grasping my bicep. "People down here drive just like they do in DC, except there they usually yield to pedestrians in a crosswalk."

"Different jurisdiction, different traffic rules," I said. "Guess we'll just have to be a bit more alert when we walk."

As the black car receded in the distance I noted the North Carolina 'First in Flight' license plate. But, it was the logo on the trunk that caught my eye. I couldn't read all of the words on the oval symbol, just to the right of the license plate, but one word caught my eye – 'Rockville.' I squinted to get the number on the plate; NOV-387. Come Monday, I planned to pay a call on the local law.

Charles Ray

5.

The beach was almost empty of people when we arrived. There were only a few hangers-on sitting on the sand watching the Atlantic surf ebb and flow, and a hunched old man with a metal detector walking back and forth along the beach looking for lost valuables.

The sand made crunching sounds as we walked, and the sound of the surf as it lapped at the beach was like a large palm frond flapping in the wind. The sky overhead was blue, lighter near the horizon, with a handful of fluffy white clouds that looked like lambs playing tag with each other. Sandra took her sandals off and let the sand scrunch up between her toes. I hate that feeling, so I kept my shoes on, even though I knew it'd be hell getting the gritty sand out of the crevices later.

We walked down toward the water until we came to the line where the white sand was tan and glistening, marking the water line, and stood there letting the breeze caress our faces.

Off to our right, a sea gull flew low over the white-specked green water, and then did a kamikaze dive, emerging in a few seconds with a large fish in its claws. The hapless fish flapped, but to no avail, as the gull soared high and veered left over the beach and toward the buildings that lined the road that ran parallel to the beach. A couple of kids out with their parents jumped and pointed as the gull flew. I have nothing against sea gulls, but I felt sympathy for the fish. I'm always rooting for the underdog.

I felt the presence of the old man long before I heard the crunch of his feet in the sand. Looking to my right, I could see him, about twenty feet away, walking steadily toward us. He alternated between looking at us and down at the sand over which he fanned the circular plate of the metal detector. When he was about ten feet from us, he switched off the device and walked directly toward us. At five feet I picked up his odor – the smell of stale tobacco smoke and the dustiness of a closet in which someone had liberally sprinkled mothballs. His face was a network of parched, sunburnt flesh and broken capillaries, and it looked like he hadn't shaved in several days. The lines on his face were like a crumpled map of places he wished he hadn't been. Watery brown eyes regarded us thoughtfully. He wore scuffed black army boots, white and gray patches showing where the leather had worn away; dark blue denim pants, the left leg about an inch longer than the right; and a faded army field jacket over a gray shirt with a frayed collar. A green and black camouflaged boonie hat, the stiffness long gone from its brim, was crammed down on his head.

"Howdy, folks," he said in a voice that was surprisingly mellow and strong considering his dissolute appearance. "Y'all just come to town, didn't ya?"

When he spoke, I could see that his teeth were all stained yellow, and some on the upper right side of his mouth were missing. Sandra moved in closer to me, her body pressing lightly against mine. He looked harmless, but she wasn't taking any chances. I stood with my muscles loose, but ready to move if his appearance of harmlessness was just that – an appearance. I only had to worry about the metal detector he carried, not much of a weapon, but if you get hit with one it could do damage. I had not doubts, though, about being able to handle him.

"Yeah, just got in a couple hours ago," I said. "Thought we'd enjoy the sunset and the beach before supper."

"That's right smart. I like the beach in the evening, after most folks are gone. I like to watch the gulls and listen to the sound of the water lapping at the sand. It's plumb peaceful is what it is. Where you folks come from?"

"Washington, DC. I'm Al Pennyback, and this is Sandra Winter."

He shook my hand, and nodded at Sandra. His palms were rough and dry, and his grip was strong.

"I'm Caleb Jackson," he said. "From DC, eh? I was up that way once, way back when I was in the army," he said. "You look like you served in the army, too. You stationed up that way?"

I'd pegged him right. He was harmless. Just an old man looking for someone to talk to. I'd been raised to be polite, and I didn't see any harm in humoring the old guy.

"Not anymore," I said. "I was in the army, though. I retired out of an assignment at the Pentagon. How'd you know?"

"It's the way you walk and hold yourself. Kind of relaxed, but alert. I figure you musta been in the Rangers."

"Special Forces, but that's close. You're pretty observant."

"I was in the field artillery. They taught us to see everything. Kinda have to if you're directing them big field pieces, you know. You see things wrong and plot the wrong coordinates on the map, them suckers put ordnance on the wrong target, it ain't good, believe me." He looked at the file folder in my hand. "I'm also guessing you're not just here for vacation, either. You down here doing some kinda business?"

"Right again," I said. "I guess the folder gave me away." He smiled his yellow-tooth smile and nodded. "I'm a private investigator. The law firm I work for is looking for a woman who is reported to have been living here in Manteo."

"A private investigator, you say? I ain't never met a private investigator before. That must be pretty exciting work."

"Not really. I spend a lot of time just tracking people down in connection with inheritance cases and the like." It struck me that this old guy, prowling the beach like he did, probably knew everyone in the area. I opened the folder and showed him the picture. "You've lived in this area long I'd reckon. Have you ever seen this woman before?"

He took the photo gingerly. His hands were surprisingly clean, considering the rest of his appearance and his treasure hunting activity. After peering at it for a while, he handed it back.

"Can't really say whether or not I've seen her before," he said. "You got a name to go with the picture?"

"Megan Sutliff."

"Naw, I been living here since I got out of the army thirty-five years ago, and I can tell you, ain't nobody named Sutliff here in Manteo. Something about her face is kinda familiar, but it being a black and white picture, I can't really tell. She in some kinda trouble?"

"No, she's not in trouble." I weighed in my mind how much to tell him, deciding that the more he understood of what I was trying to do, the more help he was likely to be. "Her father died recently, leaving her a sizeable inheritance. I need to locate her to notify her and get her to go back so the will can be settled."

"I reckon she oughta be happy to see you, then," he said.

I shrugged. Best, I thought, not to tell him that she'd come to North Carolina to get away from her family, and might not want to be found.

"You'd think so," I said. "Any help you can give me in finding her would be appreciated." I had a thought. "It's possible she's living under an assumed name, and that photo is ten years old, so her appearance might have changed a bit."

"That's for sure. Ain't none of us look like we did ten years ago. Okay, I'll poke around and let you know if I find anything. Where you staying?"

I told him the name of our lodgings. He was familiar with it.

"I'll be happy to pay you for your time and any reasonable expenses you might incur in helping me."

"Well," he said. "That's right decent of you. I'm not likely to have any expenses, but I sure ain't saying no to a little extra pocket money."

I pulled out my wallet and extracted a business card and a twenty dollar bill.

"My mobile phone number's on the card," I said, handing it to him. "Call me if you find anything."

After reading the card, he carefully put it in his shirt pocket, but shoved the money back at me.

"I ain't give you no useful information yet, so it ain't right me takin' your money."

"Let's call this a deposit against future

information," I said. "It's standard practice in my business."

"Is that a fact? I think I like this private eye business – I like it a lot." He folded the bill and tucked it into his pocket with my card.

"Be sure and call me if you learn anything, anytime day or night."

"I'll be sure to do that," he said.

He flipped the switch on his metal detector, saluted me and ambled off down the beach humming to himself.

Charles Ray

6.

Sandra and I stayed on the beach until the sun was an orange sliver on the western horizon and the shadows of the buildings were reaching almost to the surf line. The sky to our north was a light purple with orange and pink tints, and to the south a darker purple with mountain-shaped dark gray clouds close to the horizon. The wind blowing in from the water had a bit of chill to it, and Sandra had begun to shiver a little, so we headed back west to the relative warmth of the building-sheltered streets of Manteo.

We stopped at a small restaurant, *Sam's Seafood Shack*, where we had crab cakes done Calabash style – that's where they dip the cakes in evaporated milk and then coat them with a spicy breading mixture before deep frying them in oil. Along with the crab cakes, we had okra and tomatoes, fried cabbage and hush puppies, all washed down with cold beer, and followed up with overly generous servings of peach cobbler with a large scoop of vanilla ice cream on top.

After supper, we walked for an hour to work off the food, getting back to the Dew Drop Inn. An older woman, her iron-grey hair pulled back severely and ending in a neat bun, was at the reception desk. She smiled and welcomed us, and wished us a good night's sleep and turned her attention back to a small color TV on a chair behind the desk.

Back in the room, we stripped down to underwear, but both of us were still a bit groggy from the large supper, so we just lay there on top of the covers, holding hands until we fell asleep.

We slept in Sunday morning, skipping the southern breakfast, opting to start with the midday meal instead. I'd heard stories about North Carolina barbecue, and they were always bragging that it was better than Texas style barbecue. Somehow, during all my time at Fort Bragg when I was in the army, I'd managed not to try it out, so I convinced Sandra that this would be a good Sunday dinner – using the preferred southern term for the Sunday midday meal – usually served after everyone got home from church. Southerners eat supper at night, rather than dinner, something I'd never been able to explain satisfactorily to Sandra, but, she finally quit asking, and she now just smiled when I forgot and lapsed back into a southern style of speech.

At any rate, it turned out she liked it. We found a barbecue joint at 11:45, located three blocks from the hotel, run by a roly-poly black man and his diminutive wife. The man cooked, and his wife greeted and seated guests, took their orders, bussed tables, and tended bar. There was a bar down the left side of the place, from about halfway in, ending in an open kitchen where diners could see their food being prepared. Two files of ten tables, each with four chairs, occupied the space to the right. Old newspapers covered the wooden table tops rather than tablecloths. The food was brought to the table on a stack of brown paper bags, which served as receptacles for bones and napkins. There were only four other customers in the place, one lone man in the back, and a couple with a preteen girl at the front corner table. I figured it was still early, and many people were still stuffed into pews at the local churches, getting their weekly dose of fire and brimstone. We took a table near the family, and the woman came from behind the counter to take our orders.

We were at a loss as to what to order. The small woman brought us two large glasses of iced tea, and told us not to worry - her husband would prepare us a dinner we'd never forget. Sandra looked skeptical, but finally agreed. The tea was sweet – a syrupy taste that almost makes me gag – so I asked for a replacement. A white wine drinker, Sandra didn't seem to mind the sweetness of the tea, which somewhat placated the woman, who didn't seem to like customers who insisted on ordering for themselves. Frowning, she went back behind the counter and poured hot water over a couple of tea bags, waited a few minutes, and then poured the brown liquid into a glass filled with ice cubes, which she brought over and put in front of me.

We sipped at the tea while we waited for the food to

be prepared, and when it arrived, the aromas alone made it worth the wait and incurring the wrath of the chef's wife, who glared at me as she placed the food on the table. I ignored her, focusing my attention on the dishes she set out, letting the competing odors slowly invade my nasal passages. The cook had pulled out all the stops.

There were thick slices of smoked ham hock, with black-eyed peas, fried okra and tomatoes, collard greens with little lumps of fat, and thick, golden-brown biscuits the size of hockey pucks. He promised us peach cobbler for dessert. When I grabbed my knife and fork and began demolishing the ham, I got a broad smile from the cook, and a look of benign satisfaction from his wife that said she forgave me for not drinking my iced tea in the proper southern style.

For the next thirty minutes, neither Sandra nor I spoke, except to ask for a dish to be passed closer. The food was that good. When we finished dessert, we both sat back in our chairs, massaging our midsections. Sandra had a look of complete satiation on her face.

"My goodness," she said. "Do people down here eat like this all the time?"

"I can only speak for Texas," I said. "But, yes, this is pretty much what Sunday dinner was like."

"It's the same here in North Care'lina, hon," the woman said as she began cleaning the plates away. "Most folk work pretty hard during the week, so Sunday dinner's the one time you can get the family together for a proper meal."

Sandra looked at the diminutive woman with her tiny waist, and her eyes went wide.

"You mean to tell me you eat like this every Sunday? How on earth do you stay so thin?"

"Guess I just got a high metabolism." The woman laughed. "Not like my husband, there. Everything he eat go straight to his waist and backside."

Standing at the grill looking over at us, the fat cook laughed. "Yeah," he said. "But, you know you like me like this. More of me to love."

The two of them laughed and shared a look that bespoke the closeness of their relationship. I remembered when I was a kid - my parents had that kind of relationship. Sarah and I'd had that kind of relationship, and Sandra and I were building one. It was a comforting way to spend a Sunday afternoon.

"Well, Sam," I said. "You are without a doubt the best cook I've come across in a long time. That meal was fantastic."

"Thanks, friend, only my name ain't Sam, it's Chester."

I looked confused. The little woman laughed. "Sam's short for Samantha," she said. "That's me. Chester thought Sam's Seafood Shack sounded better than Chester's Seafood Shack, you know, 'cause all the words startin' with the same letter 'n all."

"He's right about that," I said. "And, might I say it's a beautiful name for a place, named for a beautiful woman."

Her brown cheeks darkened and she smiled shyly. Her husband beamed. Nothing like a little flirtation to warm up a place.

My relationship mended with what turned out to be the senior partner in the management of the place – and its namesake, we thanked them again for a fantastic meal and went back to the hotel.

The red head from the first day was on duty at reception.

"Y'all have a good dinner?"

"It was great," Sandra said. "Now, I think I'd like to go and lie on the beach for a while and soak up the sun."

"Oh," the girl said. "How I'd love to do that, but I'm on duty until seven this evening. We have towels and a beach umbrella for our guests, by the way. I'll get them for you while you go up and change."

"That would be great." Sandra was beaming. This was the kind of vacation she had in mind. I didn't have much to do, either, so we'd both get to kick back and relax.

"By the way, keep an eye out," the girl said as we turned to go. "Weather man says a tropical storm's likely heading our way and there's a thunderstorm warning for the next few days."

I was already halfway out of the reception area, and

didn't pay much attention to her. Circumstances were later to demonstrate the folly of my inattention.

Charles Ray

7.

The thunderstorm didn't materialize, so our Sunday beach outing came off without a hitch. When the sun got low and the air took on a chill, we headed back to the hotel, stopping at a burger joint along the way and buying small burgers, fries and drinks for supper. Back in the room we made a mess on the bed covering with the grease from the fries, horsed around a bit, showered, and hit the hay around ten.

I woke up at five-thirty Monday morning, slipped into sweats and sneakers and went down to the beach for a morning run. Sandra was up and had just stepped out of the shower when I got back. She was standing in the middle of the small bathroom, her athletic body glistening from the water.

"What's the program for today?" Her question came from beneath the towel tented over her head as she brushed her damp hair vigorously.

"I thought we'd have breakfast together downstairs, and then I'd find the local law and see what they can tell me," I said. "That shouldn't take me too long, so what would you like to do?"

She nodded and after finishing drying off began to pull on her clothes. I stripped and jumped into the shower to get rid of the sweat and sand. Afterwards, I dressed in jeans and a light blue short-sleeve polo shirt. I put the photo of Sutliff, along with my PI License, in the pocket of a dark blue windbreaker, which I draped over my shoulder.

The Dew Drop's free breakfast consisted of biscuits, kept warm under an infrared lamp; little packets of butter and maple syrup; boiled eggs; yogurt; greasy sausage patties, kept warm next to the biscuits, and coffee. I like meat, but, after looking at the greasiness, I passed on the sausage, wolfing down a biscuit and boiled egg instead. Sandra had yogurt. We both had coffee.

After finishing breakfast, we agreed to meet back at the inn at noon. Sandra's plan involved cruising the sidewalks, looking for antique or curio shops, while I went to the reception desk and asked for directions to the sheriff's office or the town police station.

The morning reception clerk was a guy; in his mid-twenties, with light brown hair that flopped over his prominent ears. He had a pronounced overbite, and a top lip that was slightly thicker than the bottom. When he gave me the directions, he spoke with a slight lisp, so I had to listen carefully when he said, "The sheriff's offeth ith on Marshall thee Collinth."

I didn't want to insult him, so I did the translation

in my head, and came up with, 'the sheriff's office is on Marshall C. Collins.' Then, there followed a painful session as he gave me directions to get there. I'd hoped to be able to walk, but it was clear from the way he waved his arms and pointed that it would be wiser to drive. I promised Sandra I'd be back at the hotel by lunch time.

I drove out to Route 64 and turned south, back the way we'd entered the town. Marshall C. Collins Drive was on the right, not too far from where Route 64 intersected with U.S. 264 and State Road 345. The Dare County Sheriff's Office was hard to miss. It was a sprawling two-story building with a small lake to one side and a three-story flag pole in front with a large American flag hanging limp in the humid morning air. Several white police cruisers were parked near the building, but I found an empty slot for visitors near the street.

The entrance lobby was open, with a uniformed officer sitting at a desk near the front, benches across the space from him, and a series of offices, cubicles and glass covered windows in the back. A number of people, some in a uniform consisting of beige shirt with dark brown pants, some in civilian attire, worked at the various stations, talking to visitors and taking notes. I saw no one in handcuffs, and the air of the place was quiet and orderly – the opposite of what I'd encountered during my visits to cop shops in the DC area. I approached the uniformed officer, taking out my ID. He was young and fresh faced, with a small nick on his chin that had a bead of blood at one end. He kept his eyes on me as I approached, took my ID and studied it carefully, and then looked up at me with a slight smile.

"How may I help you, sir?"

I explained why I was in Manteo, and asked to speak with whoever had dealt previously with Quincy's firm. He picked up the phone on his desk, punched one of the buttons and spoke quietly. Nodding, he replaced the phone and looked back up at me.

"If you'll just have a seat over there," he said. "A deputy will be out to speak with you."

I retrieved my ID and tried to make myself unobtrusive and comfortable on one of the benches directly in front of his desk.

For a big man he was silent. He was standing three feet to my left before I was aware of his presence. When he made a throat clearing noise, I started a little. I looked up at him – and up, and up. He had to be six-eight or nine, and had shoulders nearly three feet wide. The way his biceps and chest bulged against the brown uniform shirt, I knew he worked out with heavy weights, but the shirt also stretched across an ample paunch, so it had probably been a while. He had a round head, the shape accented by the fact that his hair was cropped so close and was such a light blond color, at a distance he'd look bald. He had wide-spaced blue eyes on either side of a broad nose with a little bump halfway down, like his nose had been broken and improperly set.

"Mr. Pennyback," he said in a deep voice. "I'm

Corporal Toby Wells. The deputy said you're down here representing some law firm up in Washington that's looking for someone named Megan Sutliff that they think lives or lived here in Manteo?"

"That's right," I said. "I'd appreciate if you could give me a few minutes."

He frowned. "I already told that lawyer, Kang -"

"Chang, Quincy Chang," I said.

"Right - I already told him there's no one by that name living in Manteo, or anywhere else in Dare County for that matter."

"It's possible she's using an alias," I said. "Anyway, I do have one other thing I'd like to run past you."

"Okay, come on back. I got a few minutes."

He turned and headed for a door in the back wall. I rose and followed.

We entered a room even larger than the reception area, with three rows of desks running to the back wall. Wells had a desk on the left, near the front. He motioned me to a chair at the side of the desk and sat down, his chair making a creaking sound.

"What is it you want to talk about?" he asked.

I took the photo from the folder and put it on the desk. He looked at it and frowned.

"I know it's only a black and white, and it's ten years old," I said. "But, if you'd just take a closer look at it. Have you seen *anyone* around here he looks like that, or perhaps looked like that ten years ago?"

He picked it up and studied it closely. Then, he put it back on the desk.

"Nope, I can't recall ever seeing anyone who looks like this."

"Well, it was worth a shot." I shrugged. "I do have one other thing," I said, pulling the paper with the license plate number from my pants pocket. "Any way to trace who this number's registered to?"

He took the paper. "You want to tell me where you got this?"

I explained about seeing the logo from a DC area auto dealer on a car, but held back on telling him that I knew the name of the driver.

He turned to the computer terminal on his desk and typed the number in. After a few minutes he nodded and made a slight humming sound.

"Something come up?"

"Yes, you could say that," he said. "Tag NOV-387 is for a black 1996 BMW registered to a Morgana Savage. The address is up on the north shore of the island, halfway to Fort Raleigh City." He scribbled the address on a yellow sticky pad and pulled the top sheet off and handed it to me.

"Do you know this Morgana Savage?"

"Can't say as I do." He tapped the keys on his

computer some more, frowning. "Nothing in our files on her. Of course, that only means that she's never been arrested. Why do you want to know about her?"

I don't like lying to a cop, but I wasn't quite ready to be too open with this one just yet.

"Like I said, I saw this car in town shortly after arriving. It had this metal logo on it, with a Rockville, Maryland dealer's name. Since Megan Sutliff's from the DC area, I figured it just possible that this person might have bought the car from her. It's a long shot, I know, but I thought it would be worth checking out."

"Yeah, I guess I can see that. So, what do you plan to do next?"

Now, that was an excellent question. Here I was, way down south in North Carolina, on an island, surrounded by strangers, without one good lead to my quarry – what would any good detective do in a case like this?

I could always cut the vacation short, and go back to Washington. I could tell Quincy that I'd given it my best shot, but couldn't find Megan Sutliff. We'd been friends long enough that he'd accept my word. He'd be disappointed, and would have to come up with some other way to get old man Sutliff's will probated, but Quincy Chang was one of the top legal minds in the Washington, DC area – he'd find a way.

Sandra, on the other hand, would be another issue. I'd been promising her that we'd spend some quality time with each other before school started, and the only way either of us could do that was by getting as far away from Washington as possible. Roanoke Island seemed to fit that bill, and she was enjoying herself. She wouldn't complain if I said we had to go back home. Sandra's not that kind of person. But, she'd be disappointed.

Finally, there was me. Was I sure I'd done all I possibly could to find Sutliff? I'd basically spent one working day, and had a few brief conversations with people who, even though they claimed to know the area, might have missed her – or just be bragging about the extent of their familiarity with Manteo and its environs. Could I convince myself that I'd done all I could to find her?

In the end, that was what convinced me to keep trying. I didn't want Quincy or Sandra disappointed with me, but I wanted to be disappointed with myself even less. I decided to give it a few more days.

"The car's still my best lead," I said. "There's a possibility that this Morgana Savage bought it from Megan Sutliff. I think I'll pay her a call – assuming there are no objections."

"Good luck with that," Wells said. "Lots of folks down here aren't all that willing to talk to law enforcement – and, you being an outsider makes it even more of a problem. As far as this office is concerned, though, there's no objection to you giving it a try."

"I'm not really law enforcement. Technically, I'm kind of an officer of the court, but I just run errands for a law firm." I gave him my 100 Watt smile. "And, I'm pretty non-threatening."

He laughed and slapped the desk with a large hand.

"Right - and I'm Tinkerbelle," he said. "Big guy like you is hardly what I'd call non-threatening. Besides, I saw the way you walked when you came in. You were in the military, special ops I'd say, and you've studied martial arts."

"You're pretty observant. Guess that goes with the job. But, from the way you carry yourself, I'd say you're ex-military, too."

He nodded. "Marine Recon," he said. "Did eight years, then got out and came home to follow in my dad's footsteps. I'm a third generation member of this force."

"I thought so. You're the second person here to peg me as former military."

"Let me guess," he said. "The other one was a seedy looking character prowling the beach?"

"That's right. Said he'd done a long stint in uniform before coming here."

"That's old Caleb Jackson. He was in the artillery. Now, you want someone to tell you about the history of this place, he's the one for that. Old Caleb treks every inch of beach, and knows the place better than anybody."

"I think I'll do that," I said. "You know where I might be able to find him this early in the day?"

"Where he usually is if he's not doing odd jobs for someone," he said. "Down on the beach looking for treasure."

"He ever find any?"

He laughed. "He's still looking, ain't he?"

I thanked him for his time. He escorted me back to the reception area and wished me luck in my search.

I still had some time before I was to meet Sandra for lunch, so I decided to drive to the beach and look for Jackson.

It was a work day and the dock area was busy, but I managed to find a parking place conveniently located to both the dock and the beach – a public parking lot with several vans and sedans, mostly with out of state plates. I a group of three empty spaces near the street, and pulled into the one farthest in. Securing the file in the glove compartment, I got out and locked the door. As I was walking away, a large blue, double-cab pickup pulled into the empty space to the left of my car, its engine growling loudly. I looked back to make sure the driver had left enough space for me to get in my car when I return. He had, so there was no danger of my scratching his finish. Turning, I continued my walk to the beach, wandering along just at the edge where the saw grass grew in scraggly groups, looking for Caleb Jackson. It didn't take long. He was sitting on the ground at the edge of the sand, watching a flock of gulls diving for fish in the surf.

I walked over and sat down beside him.

"Hey, young fella," he said. "I been nosing around, but I ain't found nothing of use for you, I'm afraid. You want that twenty back?"

"No problem, you hang on to it. I'd like to ask you a few questions if you've got time, though."

He laughed and waved his arms in a sweeping gesture.

"Time's about all I got these days," he said. "What do you want to know?"

"You must know just about everyone around these parts, I'm guessing." He smiled and nodded. "What can you tell me about a woman named Morgana Savage?"

His eyes screwed up in concentration. Then, he snapped his fingers.

"Miz Savage. Yeah, I know that name. Don't know much about her, though. She lives up on the north part of the island, on the east side. She keeps pretty much to herself, living up there in an old house that's set off from the others. Got it fenced in and everything. She's the only one up there that's never hired me to do odd jobs, and let me tell you, that old place could use some work."

"How long has she lived up there?"

He rubbed a hand across the stubble on his cheek, making a sound like sandpaper on plywood.

"Hm, well now, I don't remember exactly, but I think I probably first noticed her 'bout nine, ten years ago," he said. "Don't you go be quotin' me on that, though. My memory's not what it used to be. I do recollect that old house she's livin' in was vacant a long time, and all boarded up, then one day I see this fancy black car parked in front. Then, I don't see the car anymore, but the boards over the windows come down, so I know somebody livin' in the place."

"You have any idea where she came from?"

"Naw, not really. 'Course, she does have sort of a Yankee accent, so I reckon she's from somewhere up north. Only person I ever seen her talk to is Mike over to the grocery store. He might know where she come from."

Morgana Savage was suddenly becoming interesting for a reason other than where she might have bought her car. The time frame fit, and I trusted Jackson's take on her accent. She didn't fit the description of Megan Sutliff, but people can change a lot in ten years. I was all the more anxious to talk to the elusive Morgana Savage.

I removed another twenty from my wallet and passed it to Jackson.

"You've been a big help, Mr. Jackson," I said.

He held up a hand.

"You can just call me, Caleb," he said. "And, I ain't really done nothin' to earn that money, Mr. Pennyback. Hell, I still got to earn the first twenty you gave me."

"Actually, you did, Caleb. And, I'm just Al. My business is all about information, and you've just provided me with some valuable information. I'd say that's worth forty dollars."

He smiled, nodded, and after a heartbeat's hesitation, snatched the bill from my hand, stuffing it in the pocket of his overalls.

"Well now, I'm just full of information I reckon," he said. "So, anytime you need more, you know where to find me."

I left him sitting there gazing out at the water. The gulls had snatched several fish from the water and flown off to dine, so now he contented himself with watching a couple of boys cavorting at the edge of the advancing and retreating line of foamy seawater as their parents looked on.

The pickup was gone when I got back. I checked the left side of my Volkswagen just as a precaution, but found the finish untouched.

On the way back to the inn, I stopped at the little grocery store. The old man behind the counter confirmed Jackson's information. Morgana Savage had started buying her groceries from her store about ten years earlier – or, maybe it was eleven or twelve, he thought. Like clockwork, she came in once a week and bought just enough fresh produce for about a week. Every six months, she'd stock up on canned goods, flour and the like. He also agreed that her accent wasn't local, but had no idea where she'd come from. The years might be off, but it was close enough to make me want to know more.

Sandra was just coming down the sidewalk from the west when I pulled into the Dew Drop Inn's parking lot. She was carrying two large brown bags.

"What's in the bags?" I asked, mentally trying to figure how I'd fit them in the car with our suitcases.

She looked guiltily back at me. "Nothing much," she said. "A few curios for my students. So few of them get to travel, I thought it'd be nice. What did you find out during your snooping around town?"

I told her about Morgana Savage, and my suspicion that she was somehow linked to Megan Sutliff.

"After lunch, I thought I'd go out to her place and ask her a few questions," I said.

8.

We had a light lunch at a small café around the corner from the Dew Drop – tuna fish sandwiches and unsweetened iced tea. Sandra decided to go with me to talk to Savage. I was glad for her company.

As we drove up Route 64, Sandra fiddled with the car radio in a vain attempt to find something other than country music or religious stations. She finally found a news and weather and station – not what I would have preferred, but it did beat the nasal singing and whiny preaching of the other stations.

". . . and now, for the latest weather update, our weather central meteorologist, Rodney Clayton," a deep voice boomed from the car's speakers. "What'll the weather be like for beach goers this week, Rodney?"

"Well, Dick," a slightly high-pitched and nasally voice replied. "It's a combination of good and bad news. It's beginning to look like the hurricane season's getting off to a slow start, with nothing really significant heading our way for now. That tropical depression earlier petered out pretty quick. There's another small weather center brewing, but it's predicted to stay well south of us. On the bad news front, though, the activity over the ocean has affected the weather to our west. The moisture coming in from the ocean is hitting patches of warmth west of us which could lead to some pretty serious thunderstorm activity. There's likely to be heavy rain, lightning, high winds, and even a tornado or two in the next 48 to 72 hours."

"I guess that means we should plan to stay indoors."

"That's for sure, Dick," the weatherman's high voice said. "Especially you folks living near the coast – you'll want to take much the same precautions you'd take for a hurricane. Stock up on water, batteries, and food supplies, board up your windows, and find a secure room to hunker down in until the storm passes."

"Thanks for the update, Rodney. Folks, that was Rodney Clayton from Weather Central. I'm Dick Pepper with all the news that is the news on your all-news radio station, and -"

Sandra turned the radio off.

"Not much to listen to down here," she said.

I shrugged, keeping my eyes on the road so I wouldn't miss Elizabeth Drive, which, according to the directions the young reception clerk at the Dew Drop, was the road off which we'd find Savage's house. I don't usually try to listen to the radio when I drive.

Outside the Washington area, where reception of the public radio stations is iffy, you tend to find mostly news stations when you drive north and country music and religious stations when you drive south. In between you find a succession of right-wing talk shows spouting drivel that only the mindless listen to.

The scenery along the highway was mixed. A few small frame houses, some with well-tended front yards, others with rusted hulks or rotting tires serving as yard ornaments, and here and there a garage or gas station with rusted and fading signs. The land to the left was flat, while on the right there was a slight rise, behind which I'd been told were water view cottages and houses belonging to those who could afford the land prices. Intermixed with all this was the occasional small farm – little more than a few acres for growing corn or melons, with the excess crops peddled from small rickety stands along the roadside.

I spotted the sign for Elizabeth Drive off to the right, just beyond the big sign on the left marking the turnoff to the Dare County Regional Airport. Slowing the Volkswagen, I turned onto Elizabeth, craning to look for the right turn to Savage's place. A number of unmarked gravel roads wound into the hilly terrain, and I counted as we passed them, until we came to the fourth such lane. The tires made a crunching sound as I left the concrete of Elizabeth Drive. The road, little more than a one-lane path not much wider than the average driveway, wound serpentine like, with sandy berms on either side, behind which were stands of pine trees. We drove upwards for about a quarter mile, and then the terrain leveled off. Off to the right, I caught a glimpse of the Intercoastal Waterway between the trees. If there were houses behind the trees, they were well concealed, and the path didn't look all that used.

So, when we came to the iron gate sagging on two metal poles and blocking the road, I was caught off guard. I came to a tire crunching halt, throwing up a spray of gravel that pinged off the gate. I got out of the car and walked to the gate. It was held shut by a metal bar, but not otherwise locked, looking as if it was meant more to discourage visitors than actually keep them out. Pulling the bar from the slots holding it, I pushed the gate open. It swung inward with a creaking sound, bouncing slightly as it hit the grass-covered hummock at the side of the gravel path.

I got back into the Volkswagen and drove through the opening, stopping when I was clear of the gate's swing. I got out and reclosed the gate, putting the bar carefully back into place.

The gravel path wound upwards a bit more and swung from right to left in a lazy series of curves. As we came around the last right-hand turn, the house came into view.

At some point in the past it had been a beautiful – even sumptuous – residence, probably belonging to some rich family who used it for summer vacations. Now, though, it looked run down, and but for the curtains fluttering in the large windows to either side of the large door, could have been just another abandoned building.

It was two stories, with a porch that ran around the front and sides – and, I assumed, the back, which faced the waterway. The center portion jutted a bit higher than two stories, with a small circular window under the steep roof, which plunged down on each side to the roof covering the two sides, looking like a triangle sitting atop a rectangle. Several of the reddish roofing slates were missing, creating a black and red pattern. The wooden walls had once been a bright green, but were now a dirty greenish white with brown fungus on the south wall, and dirt stains on the front. The front and side yards were overgrown with saw grass and dandelions poking up from the reddish-brown dirt. A couple of stunted and gnarled oak trees were on the south side, and a small stand of pines on the north.

On the north side of the building was a small garage, big enough for one car. Also wood, it was the same color scheme as the house, with even more signs of wear and tear. The double doors were closed and locked with a large padlock, that was considerably newer looking than the hasp and eyebolt to which it was attached.

I parked in front of the garage and got out of the car. My feet made crunching sounds on the dry dirt that constituted the place's front lawn as I approached the front steps. As I neared, I could see that the boards of the steps were uneven, as were several of the floorboards of the porch. The wicker porch furniture was brown stained and cracked. Caleb Jackson had been right – this place was badly in need of the attention of a good handyman.

Sandra got out, waiting for me to come around the back of the car. When I approached her, she grabbed my hand.

"What's the matter, hon?" I asked her.

"Well, for starters, this place is creepy," she said. "It's like something out of the Addams Family."

Looking at the place again, I could see her point. It would be a scary place in the dark. I squeezed her hand.

"Not to worry," I said. "Ghosts don't come out in the daytime."

"Maybe ghosts need the dark, but ghosts or no ghosts this place gives me the heebie jeebies."

As if on cue, the sky suddenly darkened. I looked up. Off to the south, a mountain of dark clouds had formed, and they seemed to be heading our way. There was a slight smell of ozone in the air. Crows, somewhere in the pine trees, cawed loudly. Hell, her jumpy mood was contagious. I felt a cold tingling at the base of my skull.

But, I had a job to do.

"We'll only be here a short while, babe," I said. "I just need to ask Ms. Savage where she bought her car, and who she brought it from."

When I mounted the first step up to the porch, the boards made a creaking sound. Same for the porch – it *was* beginning to creep me out just a bit. I couldn't let

Sandra know that, though. She'd completely freak if she knew I was starting to feel antsy.

The large double doors were the darkest green of all the painted surfaces, but the paint was coming off them in large flakes, showing the bleached wood beneath. There was a large brass knocker – a lion's head with a large tarnished ring in its teeth – and a black doorbell set in the center of a large brass circle. I was debating which to try, when the door swung inward with a sound that was a cross between a groan and a slow squeak.

A figure appeared from the gloom of the room, stepping forward so that it was half lit by the now graying light of outside. Sandra gasped, and I took a step backwards.

Charles Ray

9.

"Whatever you're selling, I'm not buying," the figure said.

Her voice sounded huskier than it had in the grocery store, and she was now dressed in a black one-piece dress that touched the floor and made her look even gaunter. Her straw-colored hair hung down on either side of her head, looking like yellow spears of ice hanging from the eaves of a house. Even when she turned her head to look from me to Sandra, her hair seemed to be frozen in place. She wore a gold pin just below her left shoulder, a curved decoration that looked like the letters 'M' and 'S', which I took to be a monogram for Morgana Savage. Her lips were only lightly tinted, and she wore no other makeup, although, she had dark circles around her deep set eyes. If her hair had been black rather than blonde, she would have looked a lot like the wife in the Addams Family cartoon. It struck me that they even had similar names – Morgana and Mortitia – an odd and somewhat unsettling coincidence.

"We're not selling anything," I said. I took my identification out and held it up so she could see it.

"You might remember me. I was in the grocery store the other day. I'm a private detective, down here looking for someone."

She stared at me with eyes that were cold. I matched her stare. After a few seconds, she blinked.

"Yes, I remember you. You were asking about a woman . . . Megan something or other. I've never heard of her."

She answered far too quickly for me to accept it. She wasn't being truthful. Of that much I was certain. The problem was figuring out what she was hiding and why. I decided to press a bit.

"Our memories can often fool us," I said. "I hate to impose on you, but it's really important that I find this woman – and, the last name's Sutliff, by the way. It's possible you met her and don't remember, or that she used an assumed name."

"Uh -"

"Do you mind if we come in?" Sandra pushed forward. "It was a long drive out here, and my throat's parched. I could really use a cool drink of water."

The woman blinked again. She had that uncertain look of someone who isn't sure of the appropriate course of action. On the one hand, I figured she wanted us to get lost. On the other, southern hospitality dictated that she offer a drink of water to a thirsty stranger at her door. Sandra's trepidation over the macabre appearance of the house had been replaced with her school teacher's persona – one that was accustomed to getting what it wanted.

Southern hospitality won out over her desire to get rid of us.

"Of course," she said. "Please do come in." She stepped aside to let us cross the threshold into a large room that in this part of the country is called a parlor. The furniture, a collection of different styles, favoring flowery fabric coverings, was old but neat. The room was dimly lit by a couple of lamps on tables at either end of a three-cushion sofa with lace doilies on the arms. "Have a seat please. Would you prefer lemonade or iced tea to water? I have both."

"Tea would be fine," Sandra said.

"I wouldn't mind a glass of iced tea," I said. "Provided it's unsweetened."

"I prefer mine that way as well," she said.

She turned and strode through a door to the right. Sandra and I sat next to each other on the sofa.

"What happened to your fear of ghouls and goblins?" I punched her shoulder lightly. "You were shaking like a leaf in a high wind outside."

"Well," she said. "Your charm wasn't working on her, so I thought I'd help out. Besides, we're not outside anymore. It's a lot less scary in here."

I looked around the room. The walls were bare wood, medium brown in color. The floor was covered by a dark green carpet. In addition to the sofa, there was a kidney shaped coffee table and two cloth-covered arm chairs, both with doilies. There were no pictures on the walls. The only decoration, in fact, was a large blue vase of artificial flowers on a table near the front window. It might not be scary, but it was about as eerie as the outside had been. The effect was heightened by her choice of the long black dress and her gloomy expression.

She returned shortly, carrying a large silver tray upon which was a crystal pitcher, three tall glasses, a sugar bowl, and a long handled spoon. She put the tray on the coffee table and poured three glasses of the dark brown tea. She served Sandra first, passing the sugar bowl and spoon along with the glass.

"My guess is that you prefer your tea sweet," she said.

Sandra nodded.

"Good guess," she said. "I'm Sandra, by the way, Sandra Winter. Tall, dark, and handsome here is Al Pennyback. He's a detective, and I'm a school teacher."

Sandra was taking control of the situation. That was actually not a bad idea. She was non-threatening, and had a way of calming people and situations. With her taking the lead, we might just get Savage to give up some useful information.

"I'm Morgana Savage," she said. "So, the two of you are down here from DC?"

"Yes. Al works for a law firm. They're trying to locate this woman, Megan Sutliff in connection with the probate of her father's will. It seems he left her quite a large sum, and they need her to be present for things to be settled properly."

Most people, when you mention things like large sum of money, will react in some way – a widening of the eyes, expressions of surprise, or questions – but Morgana Savage continued to regard me with a look akin to a vulture ogling a dying animal, just waiting for that last breath.

"I still don't see how that has anything to do with me," she said coldly. "I don't know this Sutliff woman."

"You mind if I ask you where you bought your car," I said.

My blunt change of subject got a reaction, albeit slight. Her eyes widened a fraction.

"My car? Why do you want to know that?"

I had her attention. There was a hint of worry in her eyes now. I had to proceed with caution from this point, not revealing too much until I got a sense of what she was holding back.

"I'm assuming you didn't buy it new, right?"

"I . . . you didn't answer my question. Why do you want to know?"

Cagey, she was real cagey. She'd almost spilled something, but caught herself. My suspicion meter was humming at maximum decibels. This woman *knew* where Megan Sutliff was. I just had to get her to tell me.

"There's a little symbol on the rear of your car that indicates it was sold by a dealer in Maryland," I said. Got to give a little to get a little, I suppose. "Megan Sutliff's from the Washington area, so you can see that's a lead I need to check on. Did you buy your car from someone who came from that area?"

"Uh, I . . . don't really know," she said. "The . . . man I bought it from might have been from there. Now that you mention it, he did talk a lot like a northerner."

"You bought your car from a man? When was this?"

She looked up at the ceiling, laying one bony finger against her cheek. "Now . . . let's see. Might've been about . . . six . . . or eight years ago I guess. I don't remember exactly."

"You don't have the original paperwork?"

"Oh no, I only got the pink slip from him," she said. "That was turned in when I registered it and got a new title in my name."

"Would you by chance happen to remember the name of the man you bought the car from?"

She put the finger to her cheek again. This time there was a twinkle in her eye.

"No, sorry, but I don't. It's been so long."

Sandra laid a hand on mine just as I started to ask another question. I looked at her quizzically. She had a strange look on her face.

"Sorry, hon," she said. "But, do you mind if I ask Ms. Savage a question." I shrugged. "Ms. Savage," she continued. "Where are you from?"

Savage frowned, her brow wrinkling.

"Uh . . . I'm . . . from . . . Raleigh," she said. "I moved here about eight or nine years ago."

Sandra leaned forward, smiling. She squeezed my hand.

"Really now," she said. "You know, I'm no expert on southern accents, Ms. Savage, but I have been a teacher in the DC school system for over a decade, and I have a pretty good ear for speech patterns. My ear tells me that you spent a lot of your life in that area."

"Wha-, I . . . are you . . . you're not calling me a liar, are you?"

Sandra deals with inner city kids, tough but sensitive youngsters, so she knows how to call someone a liar without actually *calling* them a liar. She smiled sweetly at the scowling Savage.

"Why no, Ms. Savage," she said innocently. "I'm just saying that your speech patterns are like those of an area I'm familiar with. Have you ever lived in the Washington, DC area?"

Red spots blossomed on her cheeks. She tried staring Sandra down. Sandra gazed evenly back at her, much as she did with unruly students who tried to test the limits of their misbehavior with her. And, like those unruly students, Savage wilted under Sandra's unrelentingly even gaze.

"Uh, well . . . I did go to school there," she said. "But, that was more than twenty years ago. I graduated from Georgetown. Guess during my four years there I must have lost my North Carolina accent."

"Yes," Sandra said. "I guess you must have."

I didn't miss the sarcasm in Sandra's voice. Nor did Savage. Her brow wrinkled and she frowned.

"Are you implying something, Miss Winter?"

I'm a pretty good detective. I might not be the best when it comes to distinguishing American regional accents, but I do know when someone's on to something, and Sandra was boring in on something pertinent to the case. Little bits and pieces of it were floating around at the edges of my consciousness.

"Are you implying what I think you are," I said, looking at her intently. "Do you think it possible?"

She nodded and patted my hand.

"If you think about it, babe, it makes sense," she said. "She's about the right age. Throw in the accent, the length of time she's been living here, the car – oh, and the wig she's wearing." Savage's eyes went wide and she patted her hair. "Well, it just makes sense to me."

Morgana Savage sat there across from us, her head swiveling as she looked from one to the other, like a spectator at a tennis match. The red spots on her cheeks had gotten larger.

"A wig," I said. "Are you sure?"

"Trust me," Sandra said. "A woman knows when another woman's wearing a hair piece. That's an expensive one she's wearing, but it's still artificial. Am I right, Ms. *Savage?*"

I looked at Savage.

"Is that true? Are you wearing a wig?"

She leaned back in her chair as if I'd struck her.

"Wha- . . . why . . . how dare you . . . I . . ."

"I'll take that as a yes," I said. "I'm also guessing your real name's not Morgana Savage."

Sandra laughed and slapped my knee.

"Of course," she said. "I should have noticed that first. Morgana Savage – Megan Sutliff – the initials are the same." She pointed at the piece of jewelry on Savage – Sutliff's breast. "That way, she could keep things like that nice monogrammed brooch. I'll bet she has lots of stuff with her monogram on them. Wouldn't want to leave them behind or throw them away, but if the initials didn't match it would draw questions. Elegant when you think about it."

Sandra smiled triumphantly. Morgana Savage *nee* Megan Sutliff looked crestfallen. I should have come to these conclusions myself. All the evidence was right there before my eyes, and I missed it. I patted Sandra's hand which was still resting on my knee, and gave her a grateful smile.

Savage reached up and gingerly lifted the blonde wig from her head, and placed it on the coffee table next to the silver tray. Her medium brown hair was cut close to the skull, just as it had been when the photo was taken. Her light brown eyes regarded us sadly over a nose that was now a bit too large for her face. She had the same expression as the photo – somewhat sad, somewhat judgmental. Megan Sutliff hadn't changed much in ten years. I should have seen the resemblance to the photo even with the wig.

"I suppose it was just a matter of time until someone saw through my disguise," she said. "You're quite observant, Ms. Winter."

"That comes from hanging around this guy too long," Sandra said.

I silently thanked her for throwing me that bone. She'd done this on her own, and I had nothing to do with it.

"It won't do you any good, though. I have no intention of going back to Washington. My dear brother, Melvin, can have everything as far as I'm concerned. He deserves it."

There was a note of anger in her voice, especially when she mentioned her brother's name.

"That's your decision, of course," I said. "But,

you're turning your head on a lot of money. I can let the law firm know, and I suppose they can get your signature on some kind of paper rejecting the inheritance, but, out of curiosity, you mind telling me why?"

Now her face paled.

"N-no – I mean, it's not something I'd care to talk about." She stood, smoothing out the lines of the black dress. "Now, if you have nothing else to say, I'll ask you to please leave."

Sandra and I stood.

"Very well, Ms. Sutliff," I said. I handed her my business card. "Should you change your mind, we'll be in town for a couple more days. We're staying at the Dew Drop Inn. My cell phone number's on the card."

She looked at the card for a few seconds, and then put it on the end table, wedging a corner under the base of the lamp.

"I won't be calling," she said. "When you have whatever paper that needs signing, come back and I'll sign it." She opened the drawer of the lamp table and withdrew a ballpoint pen and a small note pad. After scribbling some numbers on the pad, she tore a sheet off and handed it to me. "That's my number. Please call before you come out."

She'd regained control of her emotions and was re-establishing control of her environment. I should have seen it that first day in the grocery store. She had that ease of command that many rich people, accustomed to having their every wish granted, have. In a quiet voice, her requests were royal commands, and it would never occur to her that anyone would refuse to obey.

I pocketed the paper, saluted her with a finger at the corner of my right eyebrow, and turned to leave. Sandra hesitated a moment, a concerned look on her face.

"If you ever want to talk," she said. "I can also be reached at that number."

Sutliff tilted her head.

"Why -?" Then her regal expression was replaced by a look of sadness. Sandra has that effect on people. "Thank you. I'll keep that in mind," she said.

10.

I stopped on the way out and reclosed the gate. We drove down the hill without speaking – the only sounds the hum of the engine and the crunch of the tires on the gravel. When we reached Elizabeth Drive, I turned right, narrowly missing a blue pickup truck that was parked on the shoulder near the turnoff to Sutliff's place. I got a quick glimpse of the pickup's driver; broad shoulders, unkempt brown hair hanging under a John Deere cap, big hands grasping the truck's steering wheel. The face was obscured by the bill of the cap.

"Damn," I said. "That's a dumb place to park."

Sandra, the fingers of both her hands digging into my right shoulder, let out a long breath. She twisted around to stare out the rear window, and made a gasping sound.

"He's turning into the road to Mor-, er Megan's house."

I looked up at the rearview mirror, just in time to see the pickup disappear behind a stand of pines as it headed up toward Sutliff's house. I pulled over to the shoulder and stopped.

"Now, that's a bit strange," I said.

I took out the paper with Sutliff's number. Taking my cell phone from my pocket, I dialed the number.

"Hello," a woman's voice said after three rings.

"Ms. Sutliff, this is Al Pennyback," I said. "Are you expecting any other company?"

"Why, no," she said. "You're the first people to come up here in years. Why do you ask?"

Warning bells went off in my head. I couldn't tell you why – call it an instinct developed after years of combat experience, the ability to know when danger's near.

"There's a man in a pickup headed your way. I assume yours is the only house at the end of your road, so he must be coming your way. You might want to lock your house and not let him in."

"Oh my, what should I do?" There was a hint of panic in her voice.

"Just lock your doors and stay away from the windows," I said. "I'm coming back up."

I broke the connection and gunned the Volkswagen's engine, cutting the wheel sharply doing a U-turn. The car swayed as I hung right sharply onto the gravel road. Sandra braced her hands on the dash, staring out the window as I hung onto the wheel to keep from skidding off into the trees that seemed to fly past on both sides.

"What do you plan to do?" Sandra asked calmly.

That's what I love about her – she's always calm, and it's as if she can read my mind.

"I'll start by trying to figure out what's going on," I said. "Although, I already have a feeling it's not gonna be good. When we get there, it might be a good idea if you stayed in the car until I get a handle on things."

She nodded and, still clinging to the dashboard, fixed her eyes straight ahead.

When we arrived at the fence, I saw the gate lying askew, knocked nearly from its hinges. The pickup driver hadn't even bothered getting out and opening it, confirming my sense that he was up to no good. I slowed as we drove past the ruined gate, stopping just short of the last turn in the gravel path.

I opened the door and got out, easing it back without closing it. As I started walking toward the edge of the bushes that lined the path, I heard the creak of Sandra's door opening, and the crunch of her footsteps on the path. I turned, frowning, but she just frowned back.

"Sorry," she whispered. "It's just too creepy staying out here by myself. I'll take my chances with you."

"Okay, but stay behind me."

Slowly, I eased up to the edge of the bushes and

peered around them. The big pickup was parked directly in front of the stairs leading up to the porch. I walked toward it, keeping it between us and the door just in case. As I got closer, I recognized the big double-cab truck that had parked near me at the beach. The hairs on the back of my neck tingled. I don't believe in coincidences. It would have to be one hell of a coincidence for the same vehicle to be here now. My worry meter was pinging loudly. I glanced at the license plate. It was a Virginia plate – one more unlikely coincidence. The chrome plate frame was from Fairfax Ford. That made three, and I was certain now that whoever was driving that pickup had been following me, and dammit, I'd led him straight to Megan Sutliff. A number of scenarios flitted quickly across my mind – all bad.

I motioned Sandra to be quiet and eased around the right side of the pickup and started toward the porch. Looking up, I was even more startled to see that the front door was hanging loosely on one hinge.

"Oh, my God," Sandra said.

It wasn't looking good, not good at all. I eased up to the edge of the porch, beside the steps, and peered through the triangular gap between the hanging door and the frame. I couldn't see any movement, nor did I hear anything at first. Then, I heard a thumping sound that seemed to be coming from the second floor of the house. I put a finger to my lips.

"I think he's upstairs," I said quietly. "I'm going in. You wait here on the porch. If you hear or see anything strange, get the hell back to the car and get the hell out of here." I handed her the keys. Her hand shook as she took them.

Just as I set myself to go up the stairs, there was a bright flash, and the world seemed to explode around us. The rumble and roar was so loud I could feel the vibrations inside my head. The thunder went on and on for what seemed like forever. I froze in place, memories of my childhood flooding into my mind. Sandra made a yelping sound and grabbed my arm, clenching so tightly it hurt. When my initial panic subsided I did a quick calculation and didn't like what I came up with. An old sergeant in my first unit after training had taught me to count between the flash of lightning and the sound of thunder to figure out how far away it was, then divide the number of seconds by five to determine how far away the lightning strike was. The flash and boom had occurred almost simultaneously, meaning the bolt had hit somewhere very near by – that gave me chills.

"Okay," I said. "We both go inside. I think the intruder's on the second floor, so stay near the door and be ready to run."

I was hoping she wouldn't have to run, though. The worst place to be in a thunderstorm is outside in the open. Grabbing her arm, I ran, nearly jerking her shoulder out of the socket, taking the steps in three bounds, and in three more was inside the parlor. Once inside, I moved to the right, scanning the room to make sure no one else was there.

The sounds from the second floor were clearer, but only a little. The thunder was coming in steady rumbles now. My legs felt rubbery, and I was breathing hard. I stopped to get my breathing under control and reestablish control over the muscles in my legs.

One of the end table lamps had been knocked over, but was still putting out a small amount of illumination. Though dimly lit, I could see the entire room. The stairs to the second floor were across the room in the back. Next to the stairs was a double-wide opening into a dining room. Through the large picture window in the dining room I could see the waterway and a strip of beach. The sky was a dark purple with billowing black clouds. An occasional lance of lightning jumped from the billows.

There was another flash accompanied by a boom of thunder that caused the house to shake, and the lights went out. From upstairs, I heard a thud and clatter, followed by muffled curses.

Now, I had a problem. I had no idea where in the house Megan Sutliff was. The fact that the intruder was still bumbling around meant he didn't either, so that was the bright side of a tarnished coin, but I had to somehow get to him before he found her. At the same time, I had Sandra to worry about. I couldn't take her with me into danger, but I wasn't comfortable leaving her alone either.

Actually, I had more than one problem. With everything else there was the damn thunderstorm.

Even though it was outside, it bothered me. The way the house shook when it thundered, and the vibrations from the wind slamming against the walls and windows. I had pictures in my mind of glass swirling around the inside if the wind tore limbs off the trees and flung them through the windows. Irrational, I know, but that's the way thunderstorms affect me.

I stood in the middle of the room and took more slow, deep breaths. This was the way I'd been taught to deal with the near paralysis caused by a phobia – breathe deeply and let your mind relax. It was a form of quick meditation, and it worked. I felt the muscles in my legs and shoulders loosen, not the laxity of weakness, but the easy limberness of an athlete about to go into competition. The cold feeling in my stomach abated. I was soon able to separate the sounds, from the loud rumble of thunder to the quieter sound of furniture being shoved around on the floor above me. I could make out the voice of a man, mumbling profanities as he fumbled around in the near dark of the second floor. Before going up stairs, I made a quick circuit of the first floor – dining room, kitchen, a large study off the dining room with a door onto the deck suspended over the beach – all clear. The way pieces of furniture were shoved around, and in some cases upended, it was clear that the intruder had done the same.

I went back to the stairs. Slowly, testing each step for loose boards, I made my way upwards, all senses alert. I went up sidewise, putting each foot against the baseboard. By keeping my weight on the end of the step, I further reduced the chance of making noise. By the time I reached the top of the stairs, my breathing had returned to normal, and the muscles in my back, arms and legs were like tingling, tight, but not too tight, ready to respond in an instant. It was a feeling I'd had many times before – just before going into combat. The thunderstorm was still there, but I'd been able to push it to the edge of my consciousness.

At the top, I paused. A narrow hallway extended to my right and left. To the left was what looked like a sun room or second floor screened in porch. The door was flung open, and a wicker table lay upended in the center. Just to be safe, I walked quietly over and peered inside. From left to right, large windows from ceiling to within three of the floor were set in the wall. The windows swung inward, while the screens on the exterior swung up. A loose screen was flapping up and down and making a sharp slapping sound as it hit the window frame. The room was bare – the upended table, four chairs, and a smaller side table upon which was a broken blue and white vase. I backed out, pulling the door shut slowly until I heard the bolt click.

I turned and looked down the hall. With the sunroom door closed, there was little light, but it had dampened the sounds from outside a bit. The sounds of furniture being shoved around were coming from a room at the end of the hallway on the right. Keeping against the left wall, I started toward the sounds.

I came to a door in the left wall. It was ajar, so I slowly pushed it inwards and peered into a small bedroom. There was a small, single bed; a dresser; and a night stand. The covers had been ripped from the bed and left strewn on the floor, and all the drawers in the nightstand and dresser were open, with the contents on the floor with the bed coverings. Opposite this room was another door. I opened it to find a linen closet with its contents rumpled. That left one door at the end of the hallway on the right. It was open, and the sounds of cursing and things being shoved around came from within the room. I eased up, crossed the hall and stood to the right of the door.

Slowly, ever so slowly, I peered around the edge of the door frame, looking into another bedroom. The covers of the large, queen-sized bed were rumpled, and I could see clothing scattered about the floor. A lamp on the wooden nightstand below a large, single-pane window was on its side. Easing around more, I could see an open door in the wall opposite the bed. Clothing, some on hangers, was being flung out into the room. I eased into the room and began to walk quietly toward the open door. Next to it was another door, slightly ajar. Through the slit I could see a tile floor and the edge of a bath tub. A crumpled plastic shower curtain lay on the floor.

When I was about three feet from the open door, a hulking figure emerged.

The pickup truck driver, his John Deere cap pulled low over his eyes, stared at me for a few seconds. His mouth gaped open.

We stood there for a few seconds staring at each other.

We both moved at the same time – he leaned over and lifted the leg of his overalls, displaying a sheath strapped just above his ankle. With a smooth motion, he slipped a Bowie knife from the sheath and, bending forward at the waist with his right hand thrusting forward, stabbed at me.

I planted my right foot flat, swung the left foot back about six inches, and shifted my weight to my left side. As the knife swished past, only inches from my gut, I grabbed his wrist with my left hand, the thumb on top, and pushed down. At the same time, I brought my right leg up sharply, slamming his right forearm across my thigh with as much force as I could. The bone in his forearm snapped like a dry twig. As his upper body pivoted forward, I jammed my right elbow in his solar plexus.

"What the fu-, ow-w-w, unnh!" The sounds tumbled from his mouth in rapid succession. The knife, a nine-inch blade with a staghorn handle, dropped from his limp fingers.

He should have been out - or at least down, but this dude was tough. He was gasping for breath, but still managed to cuff my right ear with his left fist, causing me to stumble backwards. My right ear hurt like hell. I shook off the pain. I dropped to one knee, putting my hands on the floor for balance. As I was pushing myself back to an upright position, he shook off the pain in his broken right arm, and reached down with his left hand to retrieve the knife.

As he stood, raising the knife to strike at me, I

whipped my hips around and kicked with my left foot as hard as I could. Striking him just below the spot where I'd elbowed him. He made a 'whoofing' sound and stumbled backwards and to the right.

He crashed into the window shoulder first. His feet slipped and his body slid downwards, pulling his head into the frame that was ringed with broken glass, sending shards of razor sharp glass flying. The sound of thunder and the roar of wind were like a dozen freight trains, and the wind whipped the curtains to and fro. As tough as he was, he couldn't ignore the pain of the broken forearm when he tried using it to balance himself. He yelped as his weight came down on the arm and it folded. He crashed down, his head striking the window ledge outside.

He whimpered in pain, and didn't move for a second. Then, there was a spurt of blood from his neck which was across the window pane, and his body shook. He dropped the knife and used his left hand to pry himself up. As he did so, a fountain of blood gushed from his neck, where a long piece of window glass still protruded. From the flow, I knew he'd cut the carotid artery in his neck. It took a heartbeat for him to realize what I knew in an instance – he was rapidly bleeding out. His once ruddy complexion was turning pale before my eyes. He managed to get completely upright, but his body swayed like saw grass in an ocean breeze. His arms hung limply at his side. The blood spurted from his neck with each beat of his heart, but each spurt was weaker than the one before. Finally, the spurting stopped. His heart had stopped beating. I watched the life fade from his eyes. His muscles held him upright for several seconds, and then finally gave out. He toppled forward on the floor, causing it to vibrate when his head hit it with a dull thud.

I've watched people die before – even had a direct hand in that process – but, it never gets easy. I stood there frozen, looking down at his still body face down on the floor in a thick dark pool of congealing blood.

The flash-boom of a nearby lightning strike jerked me out of the semi-daze I was in.

There was no need to check. I knew the guy was dead; dead before he hit the floor; but, I checked anyway. I felt for a pulse on the side of his neck opposite the jagged piece of glass. Nothing. Now, I had to find Megan Sutliff.

11.

I left the bedroom. Just outside the door I stopped and waited for another rolling boom of thunder to subside.

"Megan, Ms. Sutliff," I called loudly. "Where are you? It's Al Pennyback. It's safe now."

I heard a scratching sound above me. Looking up, I saw a trap door opening downward from the ceiling at the end of the hallway. When it was fully open, a set of metal collapsible stairs dropped until the end reached the floor. Her feet appeared first as she backed down the stairs. When her head appeared, she looked at me over her shoulder. Her eyes were wide and her face was pale.

"T-that man broke the front door," she said. "I just managed to get up the stairs and into the garret room before he came up here. W-what was he after?"

At that point sparing her feelings was the last thing on my mind. The damn thunderstorm was still raging outside, and with the danger of ending up on the point of a Bowie knife gone, my mind was back on my fear of storms.

"If I had to guess," I said. "I'd say he was here to kill you."

She dropped the last two feet to the floor and clapped her hands over her mouth. Her eyes got wider and her face went fish belly white.

She looked past me at his body on the floor. At some point before he fell, he'd turned slightly and the blood had spurted a long red slash across her bed. I hadn't noticed that little detail.

"Oh, my God," she said. "What a mess. Is he dead?"

"Yeah, he's dead. Before we got here, did he say anything? Have you ever seen him before?"

She looked from the body to me.

"No, I mean, he was cursing like a drunken sailor," she said. "But, he didn't say anything useful, and, no, I've never seen him before. Why would you ask that?"

"His pickup has Virginia plates, and he bought it in Fairfax," I said. "That's too much of a coincidence for me. I think this guy followed me down here from DC, waiting for me to lead him to you so he could kill you. You know anyone in DC who wants you dead?"

She blinked a couple of times.

"No, I don't," she said. "I left Washington a decade ago, and haven't been back. When I lived there, I stayed out of the public eye, and never had much involvement in my father's company, so I can't think of why anyone would have anything against me."

It came pouring out, and the only part I believed was about her leaving Washington and not going back. How, you might ask, did I know she wasn't being entirely truthful? She told me too much. When people answer a simple question – 'You know anyone in DC who wants you dead?' – with that much detail, they're either blowing smoke up your skirt, or there's something they don't want you to know and they're hoping you'll focus on the details and stay away from it.

I tried telling myself that it was none of my business. My job was to talk her into going back to DC for the probate hearing, or, failing that, find out from Quincy what other action would be needed. I didn't convince myself. If someone wanted her dead, it didn't seem likely they'd give up just because the first hit man failed. Then, there was the fact that I'd been used to get to her, and that pissed me off. I decided not to press her on it. After all, she had a dead body in her bedroom, and had I not returned when I did, that body just might have been hers.

"Okay," I said. "We need to call the local cops, though."

She looked at the phone on the bedside table – next to the bed with the large blood stain.

"We can try the phone in the parlor," she said.

I followed her downstairs. Sandra was standing in the corner of the parlor where I'd left her. Every time there was a crash of thunder, she jumped.

"W-what happened up there?"

She must have heard the window break. I told her what had happened. Her face paled.

"Now, Ms. Sutliff," I said. "I think it would be best if *you* were the one who called the police."

She picked up the handset of the phone on a credenza near the stairs and held it to her ear. She frowned. Reaching down, she tapped the cradle several times before slamming the phone down in frustration.

"The line's dead. Guess the phone lines went down with the power," she said.

I took out my mobile phone and tried dialing 911. All I got was an earful of static.

"I'm not getting any reception either," I said.

"That happens during storms down here," she said, shrugging. "Wind might have knocked a tower down. It'll come back when the storm's over."

Sandra walked over and linked her arm in mine.

"You mean we have to stay here with a corpse, no electricity, and a corpse until the storm ends?"

I patter her hand.

"Don't fret, sweetheart," I said. "Right now, this is the safest place to be. A dead man can't hurt us, but if we go out in that crap, lightning can."

She didn't look convinced. I led her to the sofa and pulled her down next to me, wrapping my arm around her shoulder. Megan Sutliff sat in the chair opposite us. Some of the color had come back to her face.

"He's right you know," she said. "This old house is built to withstand hurricane force winds. We're okay as long as we don't get too close to a window. You definitely wouldn't want to be outside right now, though."

Sandra sighed and laid her head on my shoulder.

"Some vacation this has turned out to be," she said.

Charles Ray

12.

The storm lasted another hour, and as quickly as it had started, it stopped.

It was like someone had thrown a switch. The rumble of thunder just stopped, and the lead-gray sky turned a bright blue. We could hear the squawking of gulls, back from wherever they'd sheltered during the storm, again diving for fish in the shallows of the waterway. It was as if there'd never been a storm. I think sometimes that freaks me out even more than the storm itself – the way things can change so quickly. The world sounds like its crashing in around your head, and it just goes quiet. The smell of ozone in the air evaporates, the clouds disappear, and the birds and animals come back from wherever they hide during storms acting as if nothing happened. It reminds me of just how fragile we humans are, and how subject to the whims of nature – and how capricious nature can be.

I had to go back to the second floor and stand near the window of the sun room, but I managed to get a signal on my cell phone and got through to the sheriff's office. I asked the operator to put me through to Corporal Wells. Having a corpse on the premises was going to be enough trouble without my having to explain it to a total stranger.

When Wells came on the line and I told him what had happened, he told me not to touch anything until he arrived. I went outside and moved the Volkswagen, which I realized was blocking the narrow lane, parking it as far from the pickup as possible.

It took Toby Wells, accompanied by a forensics team and another uniformed deputy, forty-five minutes to arrive. They were followed shortly by an ambulance with an official from the coroner's office.

I met them on the porch.

"Where's the stiff?" Wells was all business.

"Upstairs, last room on the right," I said.

He turned to the others and motioned them in.

"Now, you want to tell me what happened?" He took a notebook and pen from his shirt pocket.

I gave him all the details, right down to the fight, and my suspicions about the dead guy.

"You went up against a guy wielding a knife with your bare hands," he said, shaking his head. "You're either pretty gutsy, or pretty stupid – no offense meant."

"None taken," I said. "I was trained well in the army, and he was clumsy."

"So, you think he was here to kill Ms. Sav-, er Ms. Sutliff? Geez, she's been right under my nose all this time."

"It's the only thing that makes sense. He has Virginia plates, so it's unlikely he's a run of the mill home invader."

"I think you're right," he said. "Hopefully, we'll be able to identify him and confirm that. I don't see any holes in your story, but I will have to talk to the two ladies just to cover all bases. Hope you're not planning to leave town for a day or two? Not that you're suspected of any wrongdoing, but until we wrap the case up, I really need to be able to tell my boss I know where all the witnesses are."

I didn't mind. The guy was being so damned polite, and I could see his point. He was certainly a lot more considerate than most of the cops I've encountered.

So, I'd done what I'd been paid to do. I'd found Megan Sutliff. There was still the matter of whether or not she'd go back to Washington, but I was pretty sure Quincy would work that out. I didn't think he'd mind me hanging around on the firm's dime for a few more days.

I waited on the porch while he went inside and talked to Sandra and Megan.

It was well after dark by the time the cops were finished and the body had been put in a body bag and hauled away. Megan Sutliff, who by now had insisted I stop calling her 'Ms. Sutliff,' decided that there was no way she could spend another night in the house after what had happened, so I called the Dew Drop Inn and, learning they had a couple of vacancies because of last minute cancellations, booked her a room – fortunately in a wing of the building opposite Sandra and me. She threw some clothing and makeup in a travel bag, tossed that in the back of her BMW, and followed me back into town.

Sandra had suggested that we all get together for a late supper after Megan had checked in and cleaned up, so at nine, I found myself sitting with them at the seafood restaurant we'd eaten at our first night in Manteo, nursing a Corona and waiting for my crab cakes to be done. Sandra and Megan were sipping at white wine. It had been a hell of a day, but the color was back in their cheeks, and I was finally over the storm.

I noticed that Sandra was looking at me strangely over the rim of her wine glass.

"What's up, babe? You look worried," I said. "The worst is over now."

She put her glass down and reached across the table, laying her hand on mine.

"Al, I've been with you for a long time now," she said. "And, I've seen you face danger without flinching." She traced a circular pattern on the back of my hand. "I . . . hell, there's no easy way to say this, so I'll just blurt it out. Today, as you went up those stairs, I'd swear I saw fear in your eyes."

I'll give Sandra this; she might not be a detective, but she's pretty damned observant. Of course, in order to be successful as a teacher in an inner city high school, you do need to have eyes in the back of your head. I'd shared a lot with her, but this was one of my dirty little secrets that had never come up before. I'd come to a point in our relationship, though, where I felt it appropriate to share everything. It wasn't ideal that there was someone else present, but Megan had shared the experience with us, so it wasn't totally inappropriate for her to be privy to the information. The story of being caught deep in the woods with my cousin Winston in a thunderstorm came pouring out of me like water from a burst main. When I was done, I felt lighter, as if a great burden had been lifted from my shoulders.

"You'd never know storms affected you, the way you went up against that guy with the knife," Megan said quietly.

Sandra chuckled softly. "I've seen him face even greater odds," she said. She patted my hand again, and gazed into my eyes.

She didn't have to say anything more. Her touch and look said all I needed to hear.

The waiter brought our food. I had the crab cakes with collard greens on the side. Megan had convinced Sandra to join her in having fried catfish with hush puppies and fried okra. The mood at our tabled lightened considerably.

I raised my beer glass.

"Here's to good food, and good friends," I said.

"Here's to going home," Sandra said.

"Amen to that," Megan added.

"I guess they should have your place cleaned up and habitable in a few days," Sandra said.

"Oh, not that place. That's never been *home*. It's just a place where I've been hiding for the past ten years. No, home is back in DC, and that's where I'm going, so, Al, you can call your Mr. Chang and tell him I'll be at that probate hearing."

We raised our glasses in a toast to 'going home.'

13.

Toby Wells took three days to identify the dead guy. He called the hotel early Saturday morning to inform me that fingerprint evidence had come back identifying him as August 'Augie' Small, of Falls Church, Virginia, suspected in the contract deaths of several people up and down the eastern seaboard, but there'd never been enough evidence to convict him. The police would write him off, and probably close a lot of cold cases in the process. Wells happily informed me that his boss, the sheriff passed along his thanks and regards.

The county attorney, Wells said, had read the statements taken at the scene and ruled Small's death as an unfortunate 'accident' that occurred during his attempted assault upon the occupant of the dwelling, Morgana Savage aka Megan Sutliff. Sandra and I were free to go. When I told him that Megan was also leaving, he just grunted into the phone. I took that as a 'no problem.' As soon as he rang off, I called Quincy to let him know we'd be back in DC sometime on Monday.

There was no sense fighting weekend traffic, so the three of us decided to wait until Monday morning to head back. At mid-day on Sunday, we drove back to Megan's house to pack the last of her things. The crime scene tape, along with Small's pickup, was gone, but the rancid smell of death hung in the air. We packed quickly and quietly and as I followed her BMW down the narrow gravel lane, I noticed that she never looked back.

After we got back to the Dew Drop Inn, Sandra and I changed into shorts and went to the beach. We lay there on the sand until the sun was a half-globe behind the buildings of Manteo, and casting shadows that reached us. We invited Megan to join us, but she decided to stay in her room. The three of us got together for supper at the little barbecue place run by the diminutive woman with the husband who was so fat he probably hadn't seen his feet since junior high school. If anything, the food was even better than it had been the first time we'd eaten there, and the man and his wife were overjoyed that not only had we come back, but we'd brought another customer.

After supper, we went back to the inn and turned in early.

The three of us were up the next morning before anyone else in the place, so we had the little breakfast nook just off the reception area to ourselves. We finished breakfast, went back to the rooms and got our bags, and checked out. By 7:30, we were on the road. I led the procession, with Megan following close behind in her BMW. Northbound traffic was light, so we made good time until we neared the Suffolk area, where we were delayed on I-64 by a two-car accident that shut down all but one of the west-bound lanes. The backup cleared by the time we reached the Colonial Williamsburg off ramp, and we were able to reach the I-295 bypass at Richmond by 10:00.

It took us another three and a half hours to get to Washington, thanks to the ever-present construction along I-95, and traffic backed up at the junction with the Washington Beltway and I-395 near Springfield, Virginia. After making our way through that snarl, we crossed the Fourteenth Street Bridge at 1:30. I found parking spaces near the Department of Agriculture on C Street and pulled over for a hasty conference with Megan. She agreed that we should go first to Quincy's office to check in before going to her family home on Fulton Street, just south of the National Cathedral.

The offices of Holcombe, Stein, and Chang are on K Street, between Farragut Square and McPherson Square, in one of the steel and glass towers occupied by a number of law firms and lobbyists. We parked in the basement garage. The parking fees in these places are ridiculously high, befitting the highly-paid occupants of the building, but that would be added to my expense account. The three of us then took the elevator up to the floor occupied by the law firm.

The young woman at the main reception desk recognized me and waved us back to Quincy's office, in the corner with a view of the top of the White House to the south. His personal assistant, an elderly woman with her hair dyed pink instead of its normal blue, gave me a flirty smile and told us to go right in. Quincy was expecting us.

He wasn't alone in his office.

Quincy sat, as usual, behind his expansive desk, the high-backed executive chair tilted back. His dark gray suit jacket had one button done. His tie was maroon with gold flecks and the power dimple in the knot. The shirt was a slight, very slight gray. He was, in a word, immaculate. There were three chairs to the right of his desk and one to the left. The three on the right were empty.

The man who sat in the chair on the left had a face that resembled Megan Sutliff's. Resembled in the way raisin resembles a grape. Where her features were chiseled and well defined, his were soft and mushy. Her gaze sliced right through you. He wouldn't meet my gaze. She had strong hands, tanned and roughened from exposure to wind and sun. His were pale, like the belly of a fish, and looked like they barely had the strength to pry open a pistachio nut. Her lips were firm, if unsmiling. He didn't smile either, but his lips were pouty. In other words, while she wouldn't win a beauty contest, her image was pleasant enough – she was the kind of woman some people would call handsome. He, on the other hand, looked like he'd just eaten a sour apple and found a worm in the core – not what you'd call ugly, just slightly off kilter.

"Al, Sandra," Quincy said in an overly cheerful voice. "Hope you enjoyed your little vacation." He stood and came around to the front of his desk. "You must be Ms. Sutliff. Welcome home."

I gave him a brief handshake. He kissed Sandra on

the cheek, and then grasped Megan's hand. Her eyes, though, weren't on him. They were boring through the man in the chair, who hadn't bothered to rise when we entered. There was no love in her eyes, and the return expression was one of mutual dislike.

"Thank you, Mr. Chang," she said. "Hello Melvin."

"Megan," the man said, still not rising. "Welcome home."

The temperature in the room seemed to drop several degrees. So, I thought, this is the twin brother. Except for height and a faint facial resemblance, they didn't seem to share much – certainly there was no evidence of any affection for each other.

"Al, this is Melvin Sutliff, the other party to the will," Quincy said. "I asked him to join us. I hope you don't mind, Ms. Sutliff."

"It doesn't really matter to me," she said. Her expression said it did matter.

"I'm surprised you even came," Melvin Sutliff said. "You didn't even bother coming to dad's funeral."

She stiffened and balled her fists up. For a second it looked as if she'd slug him. Then, her expression softened. "I heard about his death too late to get here for the service. Besides, it was probably better for me not to be there."

He made a sniffing noise. "I'm sure he would have wanted you to be there."

Her face turned red and she wrenched her gaze away from his.

"Well, why don't we all have a seat and get down to business," Quincy said. He had a harried look on his normally placid face.

This wasn't a place I particularly wanted to be. The business of the rich, as far as I'm concerned, can remain theirs alone. I have no desire to become involved. I'd already done my part – I got Megan to return to Washington. My presence didn't seem particularly useful, or appropriate.

"Why are Sandra and I here?" This didn't seem like any business of ours. "This is family business."

"I'd rather you stayed," Megan said quickly.

Quincy held up a hand. "If there are any documents signed, we'll need witnesses," he said. "Technically, you're not an employee of the firm, so you and Sandra are truly disinterested parties. Now, Ms. Sutliff, I've already talked to your brother, but I'd like to tell you the provisions of your father's will."

She sat in the chair farthest from her brother. Sandra sat next to her, leaving me the chair closest to his. Even the width of the desk wasn't enough for me. She clearly didn't like him, and the longer I saw the smirking expression on his pale face, the more I understood why – or, so I thought.

Quincy went through the provisions of the elder Sutliff's will, reading from a sheaf of legal sized documents. Megan's expression never changed, even when he mentioned the value of the estate. Melvin's gaze never left his sister. There was something in the look he gave her. I couldn't quite identify it – hate, envy, I wasn't sure, but whatever it was, it was strong.

When Quincy finished, he put the documents down and looked across the desk at Megan. "That's it. Do either of you have any questions?"

"Let me see if I understand this," Megan said. "The estate is to be divided evenly between the two of us?" Quincy nodded. "That means we share the running of Sutliff Pharmaceuticals?"

"That's my understanding," Quincy said.

"That'll never work," Melvin said. "There can be only one boss of a company. Divided leadership will ruin it."

"On the contrary; the wrong leadership can ruin it." Megan's tone was frigid. "What the company needs right now is some enlightened leadership."

For the first time, color came into Melvin's pale face. He gripped the arms of his chair so tightly, though, his knuckles turned almost as white as the papers on Quincy's desk. His lips quivered as he leaned forward. "How dare you. You walked out ten years ago and never looked back. I've been the one to keep the company afloat all this time, especially in the last five years with father's health failing."

Megan copied his leaning motion, her face rigid with barely suppressed anger. "You're wrong there, dear brother," she said. "I've looked back many times, and frankly, I've not been impressed with what I've seen."

He took a deep breath and settled back in his chair, a strange look on his face.

"If that's so, why did you even bother to come back? You've never shown any interest in the company – even before you ran away. Do you think the company's in some kind of jeopardy, and that you're coming back to save it?"

"No, Melvin," she said. "I came back to save myself."

The pink circles on his cheeks flamed brighter, and his eyes narrowed into slits. The quivering of his lips was more pronounced now, and a small thread of spittle leaked from the left side of his mouth.

Quincy had been looking from one to the other, tense in his chair. I had to admit to a bit of tension myself. There was a moment when it looked as if Megan would leave her chair and launch herself at her brother's face. In a stand-up fight, my money would have been on her, but I wouldn't have been able to sit and do nothing, if for no other reason than I owed it to my friendship with Quincy to help maintain decorum in his office. I leaned forward, ready to grab her if she moved.

A good man in a tight situation, though, Quincy stepped in when it looked as if the temperature had almost reached a boiling point. He didn't raise his voice – in fact, he spoke so quietly we all had to crane our heads to hear him – but, he got everyone's attention.

"I think the discussion of how the company should be run would be best tabled until another day," he said. "Right now, I need to prepare for probate. Am I to assume that both of you are satisfied with the terms of the will?"

"Yes, I suppose so." Megan relaxed. "We should respect the old man's last wishes. You prepared the will, did you not?"

"Yes," Quincy said. "The current version was executed six years ago."

Melvin Sutliff turned his attention to Quincy. "Are you sure he was fully competent at the time? He had his first stroke about that time."

Quincy's expression was mildly disapproving. "Despite his physical problems, he was in complete control of his mental faculties. Are you planning to contest the terms?"

There was no mistaking the tone of Quincy's voice. His voice was level, but there was a hint of anger in the precise way he pronounced each word. His integrity as a lawyer was being challenged, and he was pissed. Quincy's no model of the inscrutable Oriental, having been born and raised in southern California, but he knows how to keep his feelings in check. I've often wondered what it would be like if he ever blew his top, and the way Melvin Sutliff was goading him, I was silently betting this might be the day I'd find out.

Like most bullies, though, Sutliff was mostly talk. When the target of his chiding stood up to him – even quietly – he backed down. "No, I don't suppose that would do me any good. I was just curious."

Quincy carefully picked the papers up, straightened them, and placed them in a manila folder. "In that case, there's nothing more to do but let the probate court know and await their decision. That should happen by the end of the week." He looked at Megan. "Ms. Sutliff, you've been away for some time. Have you a place to stay?"

"I was hoping to stay at the only home I've ever known, the family house on Fulton Street." She looked coldly at her brother. "That is, provided I'm still welcome."

"Knock yourself out," Sutliff said. "I've been living in a suite at The Watergate for the past five years. The old place has been empty since father died. I let the household staff go, except for the groundskeeper who makes sure no one breaks in. I'd been planning to put it on the market, but since you're now half owner, you might as well stay there. I would think though that you'd want to sell it – considering."

He left a lot unsaid. Megan's face darkened, and she clenched her fists.

Sandra laid a hand on her arm. "We'll go up with you and help you get settled," she said.

She grasped Sandra's hand, a mixture of gratitude and – fear? – on her face.

"T-thank you," she said. "I'd like that very much."

Charles Ray

14.

Quincy thanked me for finding Megan. Melvin Sutliff gave me a cold look and didn't offer to shake hands as we left. The pink-haired personal assistant took our garage tickets and stamped them, running her gnarled forefinger around seductively on my palm as she returned mine. On the way down in the elevator, Sandra kept nudging me and smiling, which caused Megan to ask why, whereupon Sandra told her about the finger play. By the time we got to the basement parking garage, we were all laughing. Megan wasn't half bad looking when she laughed, and it seemed to relax her. By the time we got to our cars, the tension I'd noticed in Quincy's office seemed to be gone.

I let Megan drive out first so that she could lead us to her house. She turned right on K Street and right again on Connecticut Avenue. We went through a snarl of traffic at Dupont Circle, exiting onto Massachusetts Avenue heading northwest. After Sheridan Circle, the traffic thinned out considerably, probably because once you cross Charles Glover Bridge over Rock Creek, you're approaching the U.S.

Naval Observatory, which is home to the U.S. Vice President, and while it doesn't have quite the security of the White House, there are enough Secret Service agents, in plain clothes and uniform, around to make you not want to loiter. A few blocks past the observatory, we made a sharp right onto Fulton Street, and drove left through an opening in a large black wrought iron fence just before Thirty-Fourth Street. The pebbled driveway was wide enough for two cars, and just beyond the open iron gate, a rusty brown Toyota pickup was parked. Megan drove by without noticing, so I guessed the pickup must belong to the groundskeeper.

The area behind the iron fence was larger than it appeared from the street, stretching back almost to Garfield, the street north of Fulton. Stately oaks and elms were planted in such a manner as to keep most of the area in shade regardless of the position of the sun. Beneath the trees, English ivy, azaleas and hyacinths were arranged in pleasing groupings, with small white iron benches near each group. Gray stone bird baths were set a few feet from each bench.

From the street, you could just see the right side of the house and another building to the right of that. The rest of both structures were hidden from view by the trees and dense shrubbery around them.

Megan followed the drive up to a two-story house constructed of two different types of stone – irregular multicolored stones covered the first floor, and red bricks the second. The roof was dark gray slate. The covered front porch, with stone flooring that matched the first floor exterior, took up half the width of the house and wrapped around to the right. A stone walk curved from the driveway to the wide stone steps. The chimney on the left side jutted six feet above the peak of the roof. The other building, a red brick semi-detached garage sat on the right, connected to the house by a covered, glass-enclosed walkway. She parked her BMW near the steps, and I pulled the Volkswagen in behind her.

As we got out of the cars, a hunched over old man wearing faded blue jeans, a dirt-stained brown shirt, and a broad brimmed straw hat, came around the side of the garage carrying a straw basket containing twigs and leaves. When he saw Megan, he dropped the basket and ran over embracing her. She hugged him back, not seeming to mind that dirt from his trousers was getting on her blue knee-length dress. When she released her hug, he stepped back and removed his hat. His hair, jet black with a scattering of white, flopped down to touch his bushy brows and covered his ears. He had high cheekbones, a sharp, straight nose, and a broad forehead. His skin was the color of a bronze carving. There were tears in his dark brown eyes as he gazed up at Megan, who was about six inches taller.

"Senorita Megan," the man said. "It is so good to see you back again. I am so sorry about your papa."

He bowed his head and crossed himself. Megan brushed idly at the dust on her dress.

"It's good to see you, Miguel," she said. "How is

your family?"

"Oh, they are fine, senorita. My Paulo now has three sons, and Maria will soon marry." He put the hat back on, looking now like a gardener instead of a bronze Aztec statue.

She turned to Sandra and me. "Guys, this is Miguel Fuentes," she said. "He's been the groundskeeper here for as long as I can remember. It was Miguel who taught me how to climb trees and how to catch fireflies. Miguel, this is Ms. Sandra Winter and Mr. Al Pennyback. They came all the way to North Carolina to bring me back home."

Fuentes touched the brim of his hat and bowed toward Sandra. He extended a sun-bronzed hand to me. *"Con much gusto, senorita y senor,"* he said. "Thank you for bringing the senorita home."

His grip was firm, and he locked eyes with me as we shook.

"If I know you, Miguel," Megan said. "The inside of the house is as clean and orderly as the outside."

"Of course it is." He stood with his chest out and his shoulders back. "I go inside once each week and make sure all is in order. Always, though, there is dust. You know the *patron* always insisted on everything being kept in order. Will you be staying now? Your papa, he always talk about you and how he hope you would come back someday."

Megan's face clouded, but she quickly recovered, and smiled down at him. "Yes, Miguel, I'm back to stay." She turned to us. "Can you guys help me get my stuff inside?"

"I can do that for you, senorita," Fuentes said.

"No, that will be fine, Miguel," she said. "We can handle it. Come on in, guys, and I'll fix us some lunch – I'll fix some for you too, Miguel."

"*Gracias,* senorita - that would be nice." He touched a finger to his hat brim and turned and picked up the fallen basket.

She opened the trunk of the BMW and I started hauling out her cases and boxes. In the meantime, she and Sandra started moving things from the back seat. She had us dump everything in the living room. I felt a bit uncomfortable doing that. The living room was white – white marble floors, white ceilings, and white walls of some other kind of stone; white furniture, including a white leather L-shaped sofa that was big enough to seat ten people, a white stone coffee table and white leather arm chairs that matched the sofa. Expensive looking oil paintings at intervals on the walls added a touch of color. It was like a surrealistic museum. The untidy stack of suitcases, boxes and dumped clothes on the floor near the sofa seemed an intrusion. But, Megan Sutliff didn't seem to mind.

"You guys have a seat." She pointed to an off-white credenza to the left of the sofa. "There should be liquor in there," she said. "The right side of the credenza's a fridge, which should have beer and white wine – assuming Melvin left any when he moved out. Help yourself, while I go see if Miguel's kept the kitchen larder stocked. I'll fix us some lunch."

"I'll help you," Sandra said. "I don't really feel like drinking anything but water right now."

I passed as well. I'm not a wine drinker, and I didn't think any beer left in for longer than a week or two would be drinkable.

I made myself as comfortable as I could on the sofa, gazing out the large front window while the two of them went off toward the back of the house where I assumed the kitchen to be. I'm by nature the inquisitive type, but I'm never completely comfortable around rich people – nor do I particularly like being left alone in a rich person's house. So, I didn't snoop as I usually would. I just sat there waiting for them to bring me my lunch so I could get out of there and back to the comfortable surroundings of my own home.

15.

It only took them fifteen minutes to get lunch ready – tuna salad sandwiches and instant iced tea aren't that much of a challenge. Sandra and I picked at our sandwich while Megan took a sandwich and drink out to Miguel the groundskeeper. When she came back, we weren't even half finished.

"Hey," she said. "You guys aren't eating. Don't tell me you don't like my sandwiches. They're my specialty, you know."

We laughed. I took a big bite of mine. It wasn't bad. She'd put dill pickles in the tuna salad, and spread mustard instead of mayonnaise on the bread, which had been toasted. Not bad at all really. Sandra took a smaller bite, chewed it twenty times, and swallowed. She then put it down and looked at Megan.

"I'm not really all that hungry," she said. "I am curious, though. Something's eating at you, Megan, and the teacher in me won't rest until I know what it is."

She'd saved me the trouble of bringing it up. I put

my own now half-finished sandwich down. "Sandra's right," I said. "I noticed the tension between you and your brother in Quincy's office. That, and your sudden decision to come back when you're clearly not all that interested in your late father's company, have me curious as well."

She looked at me over the sandwich that was half way to her mouth. Shrugging, she put it down. "I guess I do owe you an explanation. After all, you did save my life."

She took a sip of tea and then put the glass down next to her uneaten sandwich.

"I've been keeping up with events here since I left," she continued. "In particular, I've been concerned with the direction Sutliff Pharmaceuticals has been taking for the past few years. Now that I know my brother has been in charge, I understand those changes. If he's not checked, the company's days are numbered."

"Why should you care? You ran away from all that."

"That's not wha-, I mean, I do care," she said. "The company is the main source of our wealth. If it goes under, there's not much left. I suppose I could get by with what's left in my trust fund, or even get a job of sorts, but it would be a shame to let the company my grandfather built from scratch go under."

I looked around. I guessed the house was valued at a million or more, and Quincy had told me there were bank deposits totaling five or six million. I guess 'not much' is defined differently if you're rich.

So, you think by coming back you can keep that from happening?"

She gave me a defiant look. "I *know* I can. Before I left home, my father was planning for me to replace him eventually. I guess after I left he had no choice but to take Melvin into the business. My brother means well, I suppose, but he really doesn't have a head for business. He loves the perks, but doesn't like doing the real hard work."

"It's possible he's changed in the past few years," I said. "Having to step up when your father became ill put a lot of responsibility on him."

"Al, Sutliff Pharmaceuticals was started by our grandfather, Phineas," she said. "The reason he founded the company was to ensure that people of modest means were able to have access to necessary medications. He never wanted to compete with the big pharmaceutical companies – he even invested in research on orphan drugs."

"What are orphan drugs?" Sandra asked.

"They're drugs designed to treat rare and specific diseases," Megan replied. "There's usually not much profit in them, so a lot of the big companies once avoided them. In recent years, here and in Europe there have been government incentives for companies to work on them, such as those designed to deal with AIDS, for instance. When my grandfather founded the company, though, there were no such incentives, so people with rare diseases were often denied proper treatment. When grandfather Phineas died and my father took over, he continued the original policies. In the last six years or so – actually, beginning around the time I left home, the company's been focusing more on those drugs that have the greatest profit to the neglect of necessary medicines for rare diseases."

"You think this is something your brother did?" I asked.

"Of course; I know he's been the driving force behind it. My brother only cares about the money, and the things he can buy with it – none of which are intended to help others. I'm hoping that by involving myself in the company's management, I can reverse some of his venality."

"That won't be easy," I said. "He's been at the helm for long enough now that he'll have the loyalty of many of your employees – I assume you also have a board of directors?"

She shook her head. "No, we never went public. As for the employees, I would imagine Melvin's alienated many of them. You saw him in the lawyer's office. He's not exactly the warm and fuzzy type."

That much was true. I didn't want to tell her that she hadn't come across as all that warm and fuzzy herself. There was also the fact that, while she seemed to be truthful about her desire to save the company and get it back on the track her grandfather originally set it on, she wasn't telling us the real reason she'd decided to come back to Washington.

16.

"That's all well and good," I said. "But, I have a feeling it's not the only reason you decided to come back here."

"Are you doubting my motives?" Her eyebrows arched as she frowned at me. It was a good effort at an indignant response, but I wasn't buying.

She'd been through a lot, and I felt bad pushing, but something about her situation was puzzling me, and I'm a sucker for puzzles.

"No, I don't doubt that you're concerned about your family's company," I said. "But, you said it yourself; the company's been on the wrong track for a few years now. Why wait until now to come back?"

Sandra stood up and walked over to her. She sat on the arm of her chair and put an arm around her shoulder. "Ease up, babe," she said. "Megan's been through a lot."

"I know she has, and I don't think her troubles are over yet. She needs help, but if I'm gonna do it, I need to know the truth."

Megan looked at me, a hopeful expression on her face.

"Y-you'd want to help me? Why would you?"

Sandra patted her shoulder.

"Megan, honey," she said. "You've got to understand something about this man. In addition to being a pit bull when he senses information is being withheld, he has a thing about helping people in need. If he thinks you're in trouble, he can no more walk away from it than you or I could walk past a sale at Bloomingdales."

That probably describes me as accurately as anything. Lucy Mendez, a feature writer for the *Washington Post*, who has been dogging my trail and writing about my cases for years, dubbed me the Brown Knight – a nickname that's stuck. I hate it when the weak are exploited by the strong, the poor by the rich – and even though Megan Sutliff didn't qualify as poor, she did strike me as someone who felt she was going up against superior forces.

"You have something bothering you," I said. "I don't know what it is, but it's pretty big from the haunted look on your face. If you tell me what it is, maybe I can help."

Haunted was an exact description of the look on her face. She had the look I'd seen many times before in the eyes of guys who'd been on one too many combat patrols, and who couldn't get the smell of death out of their nostrils, or the images out of their mind.

"I . . . I-" Her face crumpled and tears began flowing from the corners of her eyes. She leaned against Sandra. "I've been on my own for so long," she said, when she'd regained a measure of composure. "I'm not accustomed to anyone wanting to help me."

"Get used to it," Sandra said. "You've got the Brown Knight in your corner now."

"Whatever it is that's troubling you," I said. "It can't be as bad as some guy coming into your house and trying to kill you."

She took a deep breath, and began to tell us her story. I'd been wrong. There was, from her point of view, actually something worse than some guy breaking into your house and trying to kill you.

It began, she said, when she turned thirteen. At first, it seemed innocent enough. Her father would come into her room after everyone else was asleep, and sit on the edge of her bed and talk about his plans for the future, his desire that when she was old enough, she'd come and work with him at Sutliff Pharmaceuticals, and someday would even replace him at the helm.

Heady stuff for a young girl with big ideas and dreams, who, unlike her twin brother, thought of things other than parties and buying the newest and most expensive toys, and whose main in life was to impress and please her father – an imposing figure.

At first, it was just talking, but after a few nights he

would rub her hair, or run a hand over her arms or legs. By the end of the second week, it had gone much further, and even though she knew what was happening was wrong, she'd been unable to resist. My stomach churned as I listened to her describe night after night of abuse in a voice devoid of all emotion. It was as if Sandra and I were no longer in the room with her.

At one point in her narrative, she suddenly stopped speaking, and just stared ahead, tears streaming down her cheeks. Sandra finally broke the silence.

"Did your mother know what was happening to you?"

Megan blinked, and looked up at her. "It all began the year before my mother died," she said. "By then, she'd already been sick for several years, and . . . I didn't want to burden her."

"What about servants, friends of the family, or even your brother," I said. "Surely someone must have noticed."

She was back with us now, and the pain as she remembered was clear on her face. Sandra stroked her back.

"We didn't have live-in servants, and it only happened at night," Megan said. "My mother seldom left her room. I . . . Melvin might have noticed something – his room was just down the hall from mine – but, I don't really know."

"Why didn't you tell someone," I asked, earning a

glare from Sandra.

Megan sighed. "Looking back, I know now I should have. But . . . you must understand . . . my brother and I never attended public schools," she said. "We had a succession of private tutors. We . . . hardly ever left the house until it was time to go off to college. There was . . . no one I could talk to. I . . . at first, even though it made me feel uncomfortable . . . I didn't really think it was . . . wrong. It stopped after I left for college . . . the year I turned eighteen. That was also the year I . . . my relationship with my father changed . . . I could never look him in the eye, even though he always tried to act as if nothing had ever happened. I felt so . . . guilty . . . like I'd done something wrong."

"You did nothing wrong," Sandra said. There was steel in her voice. "You were a victim, but it's unfortunate that in such cases the victim feels as if he or she is the sinner."

"I – I . . . think I know that now. That's why I left home. It was the only way I could get my sanity back. If I'd stayed here, I think I would have snapped."

"It helps to be able to talk about it," Sandra said. "And, I'm here for you if you need me. So, for that matter, is Al."

Megan had gone pale while she was recalling her past. Now, though, some color was coming back to her face. She wiped the tears away with the linen napkin she'd had on her lap. She even smiled, wanly, but smiled nonetheless. "That's reassuring – so very reassuring." She looked at me. "I do think I'll have need of your services."

"I'm willing to do whatever I can," I said. "But, I'm not all that good at psychological or emotional problems." I'd had trouble enough dealing with my own post-traumatic stress after my wife and son were killed in an auto accident. I could guess at what she'd had to go through, but I had no idea how to help someone else.

Her smile was warm. The expression in her eyes said she understood. Amazing how fellow sufferers can recognize each other. "Oh, I don't need your help for that. I think I've finally come to terms with what happened to me, and I know now that I wasn't at fault. I've even forgiven my father. With my mother's illness, and having to run the company single-handed, he too was under an incredible amount of stress. No, I need your help with a matter that's more in line with your unique skills."

That got my interest. "And, just what would that help be?"

"I think you were right. That man came to Manteo to kill me. I think someone hired him, and I don't think we've seen the end of it. I'd like to hire you to protect me."

I've done protection jobs before – they're not my favorite, ranking just behind marital infidelity cases, which I refuse to touch. "Don't you think you'd be better going to the police for that?"

"Perhaps," she said. "But, other than a firm belief,

I've nothing to take to the police. I'm convinced someone wants me dead, but I'm not prepared at the moment to reveal who. That would make a weak case for the police. You, on the other hand, would be compensated for your services."

"I take it you're not prepared to tell even me who you think wants you dead?"

"Not at the moment. I don't want to falsely accuse anyone. When the time is right, though, I promise you, I'll tell you. Will you accept the job?"

"Of course he will," Sandra said, giving me a look that dared me to contradict her.

Charles Ray

17.

Megan assured us that she'd be okay for the rest of the afternoon; Miguel Fuentes, the groundskeeper, would be there until around 6:00 p.m., so that gave me time to take Sandra to the farm house, leaving her to unpack our things, and drive to the office to check with Heather on what had happened during my absence.

I pulled into the parking lot of the building in which our office is located just after 4:00. Most Mondays the lot's full until after five, but there were surprisingly few cars. It was still warm, and with sunset in July around 9:00 p.m., my guess was that most of the other tenants had quit early burn steaks on backyard barbecues while their kids were still out of school.

Heather Bunche is not the barbecue type. She lives alone in a small brownstone house in Arlington, has never been seriously involved with anyone since I met her, and spends much of her time in the office. If anything, since she got her PI license, she's spent more time working. So, it didn't surprise me to find her bent over her keyboard when I walked into the combination reception area/office.

"Hey, Al," she said, brushing a blonde lock from in front of her blue eyes. "How was the vacation?"

"Great. Got stuck in a thunderstorm, had a guy try to gut me with a big knife, but I got the job done," I said.

I don't think she heard the part about 'getting the job done.' Her mouth dropped open at 'big knife,' so, of course, I had to give her all the details. When I finished telling her, she shook her head.

"Only you could get into that kind of trouble on a vacation."

"Hey," I protested. "It was a working vacation, remember that. Now, I got us a new client, so I need you to do some background work for me."

That perked her up. She likes doing detective work now that she's legal to do it, but what she *really* likes is coaxing information out of the ether by way of her computer. I don't know how she does it, but she can find out almost anything about almost anyone. She gets into computer files I've never heard of, in ways I don't understand, and am probably better off not understanding. Smiling, she took a steno pad from her desk drawer and sat there with a ball point poised.

"Shoot."

"Megan Sutliff's asked me to guard her," I said. "She thinks someone might try to kill her – and, after what happened in North Carolina, I'm inclined to believe it. I need you to do a full background check on her."

"Does she have any idea who might want her dead?"

"I think she does, but she's not saying," I said. "I'm hoping you'll come up with a lead by digging into her background."

She wrote Megan's name on the pad, made a little pouty face, and started pecking at her keyboard. I debated telling her what Megan had told Sandra and me about being abused, and then decided against it. On the one hand, it might not be relevant, and on the other, there was Megan's privacy to consider.

Heather stopped typing and looked up at me. "Is there anything else?"

"Uh, no, just see what you can find."

She pouted again. "Well, in that case," she said. "Would you stop standing there looking at me like a vulture waiting for something to die. A watched pot never boils, you know."

"Wait," I said. "There is something else. The real reason I came in. What's been happening in my absence?"

"Not much. Quincy had me track down some deadbeat who was trying to skip on paying his wife's alimony. Otherwise, it was a quiet week."

"I guess I can head home, then. I need to shower and change before I start my body guarding stint. I guess I'll get out of your hair."

"I thought that's what I said before," she said, and returned to her computer.

18.

What I hate about body guard work is – it's boring. It's almost as boring as stake outs. You sit around waiting for something to happen, hoping at first that nothing will happen, and then, about four or five hours into it, you're praying that something will happen.

Rush hour traffic was in full swing by the time I left the office, causing it to take me over an hour to get home. Sandra had unpacked our things and was doing laundry when I walked in.

"Hey, babe," she said. "You want a bite of supper before going to Megan's place?"

"Sure, but I'll do it. You look like you've been busy since you got home."

She leaned over and kissed my cheek. "Make it light, though, I think I put on a few pounds eating all that southern food."

I patted my midsection. We'd both probably over indulged. While she folded clothes still warm out of the dryer, I chopped lettuce and walnuts, diced some tomatoes and onions, and tossed all of them together in a large wooden bowl. I made a dressing with olive oil, balsamic vinegar, and black pepper, which I put in the fridge to chill. While the dressing was chilling, I toasted four slices of whole wheat bread and put two each on small plates. I smeared spicy mustard on all four slices, and then constructed sandwiches made of smoked ham slices, tomato slices, and spinach leaves. I'd have liked nothing better than to wash all that down with a cold beer, but I didn't want anything slowing my reflexes, so I made a pitcher of tea instead.

After a supper of sandwiches, salad, and iced tea, I gave Sandra a long passionate kiss, promised to wake her up in a pleasant way when I got home, and left for Megan Sutliff's place.

It was after 8:00 when I arrived, but the sky was still blue. Fuentes had gone home just after 6:00, but she didn't seem all that worried, saying that she didn't think anyone would make a move on her during daylight. I didn't remind her that the killer in North Carolina had struck in the middle of the afternoon. Sure, down there she'd been living in a house that was isolated from everyone, but her Fulton Street residence, surrounded as it was by trees that hid it from the street, was almost as isolated. I was in a good mood, and she seemed to be as well, and I didn't want to spoil either, so I just smiled and nodded.

"I'll probably turn in early," she said. "Would you like to join me in a cup of coffee before I do?"

"You sure it's a good idea to drink coffee just before

going to bed?"

"In college, I practically lived on coffee during exams," she said. She laughed ruefully. "I guess I ingested so much caffeine it no longer affects me."

"Well, in that case make a pot," I said. "The stuff keeps me awake, and I'll need it if I'm gonna be any good guarding you tonight."

I never developed a taste for tobacco, leaving coffee the only thing to keep me from getting drowsy. I had no desire to fall asleep on my first night on the job.

It only took her a few minutes to brew a small pot, which she brought back to the living room along with two small mugs, and two containers of sugar and cream. She put liberal amounts of both in her mug, turning her coffee a light beige color. I took mine black. She finished hers quickly. I knew that after a night of drinking the stuff to stay awake, my stomach would be rebelling the next day, so I made mine last.

She put her empty mug on the coffee table and stood. "I'll clean things up in the morning. I don't know how to thank you for agreeing to do this, Al."

"No thanks necessary, Megan. You get some rest."

"I think I will," she said. "I think I'll get my first good night's sleep in a long time."

Charles Ray

19.

The hours went by slowly. After she went upstairs to her bedroom, the place was quiet except for the occasional creaking of wood contracting in the cool air and the hum of the air conditioning unit. There wasn't much traffic on Fulton Street. Standing at the living room window I could see the occasional glow from headlights from a rare passing car, but the distance and all the foliage and trees absorbed the sound.

The house didn't have an alarm system, just smoke detectors in each room. Old man Sutliff must have relied on the proximity to the vice president's residence. A burglar *would* have to be pretty stupid to hit a residence in that area – the cops would be all over him before he could blink. Assuming, that is, there was some kind of alarm raised. I would have thought most rich people would have alarms. There was enough art alone in the place to justify it. Just goes to show, I don't understand rich folks.

I would have been more comfortable if some of the brush and a few of the trees in front had been trimmed. If someone came over the front fence, he could get within a few feet of the front of the house before someone inside would be able to see him. An intruder who worked his way around either side would be able to get right up against the house without being seen.

That made it useless to try to patrol the outside. Too many blind spots. So, I'd have to make sure to cover the inside. In order to do that, I needed to know the place cold – to be able to navigate around in it with my eyes closed.

It was going to be a long night.

I drank a mug of coffee every couple of hours, finishing the pot around 5:00. It kept me awake, but just barely. Like I said, guard duty, like a stake out, is deadly boring.

The first thing I did was check out the entire house, downstairs and up, walking through every room, opening doors, checking behind large pieces of furniture, and making sure windows and exterior doors were securely locked. I even checked Megan's bedroom. She'd been right, coffee didn't keep her awake. She was sound asleep, sprawled on her back with the covers thrown aside, snoring lightly. By now, my eyes had fully adjusted to the dark, so I was able to inspect the room without turning on any lights. Her closet was empty, as was the bathroom – which smelled of lavender – and the window was double locked.

One thing I did notice, even in the semi-darkness upstairs – downstairs, I'd turned on lights – was that everything in every room other than the living room, kitchen, and Megan's bedroom, was covered in a thin patina of dust that billowed into the air as I passed, tickling my nose. Megan had no doubt cleaned the three noon-dusty rooms, but hadn't had time to do the others.

My inspection complete, I returned to the living room. There was a flat screen TV mounted on the wall in front of the longest axis of the sofa, but even modern technology didn't alter the fact that most programs worth watching stopped being broadcast in the mid-seventies. Like radio, foul-mouthed radicals spouting absolute nonsense seemed to dominant the channels – especially after prime time.

One advantage that sentry duty has over doing a stake out, though, is that you can move around. So, I wandered around the downstairs, first checking the kitchen which was filled with all manner of cooking gadgets, and had a large walk-in freezer filled with expensive cuts of meat and frozen fruits and vegetables. Old man Sutliff might have lived alone, but he lived in style. I doubt that he'd done his own shopping. The cook, who came in every day until Melvin had fired her, was probably also the shopper, based on the 'sell by' dates on some of the frozen items. Melvin hadn't checked the stores after cashiering the household staff.

Back in the living room, I examined some of the paintings on the walls. They were all original and I guessed damned expensive. Other than the paintings, though, there were no pictures. By that I mean, no family pictures. I would have thought that a wealthy family would have one or two family portraits painted by some local artist, or a few photographs of vacations at ritzy places. But, there was nothing. I remembered that I hadn't seen any photographs in Megan's place in North Carolina either.

I was in the kitchen just before 6:00, rinsing out the coffee pot, when I heard the rattle of an engine. I looked out the window over the sink and saw Fuentes' pickup come to a stop in a graveled area behind the garage. When he got out and saw me at the window, he waved. I went to the door and opened it.

"*Jola, senor*," he said. "You have protected the senorita, no? How did your evening pass? Is the senorita awake yet?"

"Things were quiet," I said. "Ms. Sutliff is still asleep. I was just planning to get a pot of coffee going. Would you like a cup?"

"Yes, thank you, senor. That would be very nice."

While he removed some bags of mulch from his truck, I finished cleaning the pot. I found a bag of coffee in the cabinet over the sink – Colombian - measured three teaspoons into a filter and put it into the receptacle. I filled the pot from the tap and poured the water into the reservoir. Then I turned the contraption on and stood there as it began to gurgle. The gurgling stopped about the time Fuentes hefted the last bag of mulch. I got two clean mugs from the cabinet, filled them and took them outside.

"I didn't know how you liked your coffee, so it's

black," I said.

"That is how I like it," he said. He took a sip and sighed. "Yes, that is very good."

He sat on the lowered tailgate of the pickup, cradling the mug and blowing on the steaming contents. I hopped up beside him. For a few moments, we sat in silence, sipping our coffee.

"You've worked for the Sutliff's a long time, haven't you," I finally said.

"*Si, senor*, for a very long time. Since senorita Megan and her brother were little ones."

"So, you must know a lot about the family?"

He looked at me, his brows furrowed. "*No entiendo, senor.*"

"I mean, you're aware of what went on inside the house – how the family interacted with each other."

Now, he was frowning at me as he held the coffee mug up in front of his face. "I do not spy on the family, senor," he said.

"No, no." I held a hand up. "I'm not implying that, Miguel. Look, someone's trying to harm Ms. Sutliff – Megan – and, I want to keep that from happening. I think things that happened here in the past might be related. It would make it easier for me to protect her if I knew more. You understand?"

"*Supongo que si.* I suppose so," he said. "What do you want to know?"

"Was there any friction among the members of the family – say, between Megan and her brother, or between her and her father?"

His brown cheeks darkened. He gripped the handle of the mug so hard some of the contents sloshed over and landed on the leg of his blue overalls, making dark blotches.

"I . . . I don't know if I should talk about such things, senor." He crossed himself.

I put a hand on his shoulder. "Don't worry, Miguel," I said. "Whatever you tell me remains between us. I just need to have a better understanding of what I'm dealing with." I told him about the attempt on Megan's life in North Carolina. The color in his cheeks deepened.

"That is terrible that someone would try to harm her," he said. "You have risked your life for her. You are a good man, senor. There is something – I am not sure if it is why someone would want to hurt her, but I think it is why she ran away from home."

He then told me in a halting voice that he suspected that old man Sutliff was regularly abusing Megan, confirming what she'd told Sandra and me.

"Why didn't you go to the authorities," I asked. "What the old man was doing to her was illegal."

Tears welled up in his eyes, and he crossed himself. "I will never forgive myself for not doing something. I was not sure, though – it was just a feeling I had that he was doing something really bad to her," he said.

"You have to understand, though, the *patron*, Mr. Sutliff, was a very stern man. One did not go against him. Even if I had had proof, I would have lost my job. I had small children at that time, and it was difficult to find work. You understand?"

I did. It didn't make it any easier to swallow, but I did understand. Megan hadn't said it outright, but I'd already guessed that her father was the domineering type who always got his way. Even in death he was controlling her – by making her and her brothers co-heirs, he was manipulating them both.

"Surely, someone else in the household knew or suspected something," I said.

"The senora was very sick then. I do not think she knew much of what went on. I think perhaps some of the women who worked in the house must have suspected something for the same reason I did, but it would have been even harder on them. As for Senor Melvin, I think he knew just before he and Senorita Megan went off to college."

"What gives you that idea?"

"When they were small, the two of them were very close," he said. "Even though the *patron* always favored her, the boy never seemed to mind. But, the year before they left for college, I noticed that they were not as close as before. There was anger there. I thought it might be because Melvin had learned what his father was doing."

"I'd think he'd be angry at his father instead of

her," I said.

He shrugged, and spat. "Everyone always wanted to please the *patron*. I think Senor Melvin felt that his sister had found a way to please their father that was unfair because he could not. I do not know. I know only that they had a bad relationship after that. When Senorita Megan went off to college, she never came back home."

20.

My conversation with Miguel Fuentes, while it confirmed Megan's account to a degree, hadn't provided me with any new insights. I decided that I needed to get away from it for a while, so I told him I was leaving, and asked if he'd stay around until I showed up later that evening, which he did willingly.

I then drove west to Wisconsin Avenue and then north to River Road where I turned west toward home. That time of morning, all of the traffic I encountered was coming toward me, so it was a smooth ride except for the left turn off Wisconsin, which became a little hairy when a van blew a tire in the middle of the intersection, and everyone had to wait for a tow truck to pull it out. I still made it home in just under forty minutes – a record commute by Washington standards.

Sandra was in the shower, her sweats crumpled on the bedroom floor, when I came in. I quickly stripped down and joined her. I skipped my own run through the woods, and we both skipped breakfast.

At 11:30, we rolled off the bed, showered again,

dressed and made a quick lunch. I gave her the quick version of my boring night, which earned me a sympathetic nod.

"I should really check in with Heather," I said, as I finished the last of the tuna sandwich she'd quickly thrown together.

"I wonder if I shouldn't drive over and see how Megan's doing," she said. "I'm sure she could use the company."

I wasn't expecting anyone to go after Megan during the day, but all the same, I wasn't too comfortable about just her and Sandra alone in the place. Fuentes was there, but he was old, and I had no idea if he'd be much help against a hired killer. Of course, arguing with Sandra once she's made up her mind on something is like trying to put out a forest fire by urinating on it. She'd developed a liking for Megan and her maternal instincts had kicked in, despite the fact that the two of them were not that far apart in age. I could only hope I was right about anyone wanting Megan dead having nocturnal preferences, and made a note to try and get there as early as possible.

We left the house at the same time, driving in convoy east on River Road, parting at the exit for Clara Barton Parkway. I exited and she kept going. I could have gone on to Wisconsin, but the drive to my office from the National Cathedral is a lot worse than taking Canal Road past George Washington University – the latter route has fewer cars, and fewer accidents, and it's a lot more scenic.

There's a short leg on Cabin John Parkway the curves between hills on both sides that are covered with trees and wild shrubs – dangerous in fall and winter when the deer are rutting and have a tendency to appear in front of your car as you come around a curve doing fifty. Cabin John merges into Sara Barton Freeway, named for the home of the founder of the American Red Cross, whose family home is located near MacArthur Boulevard in the whistle stop town of Glen Echo. You have to slow when Clara Barton merges into Canal Road, a two lane blacktop route that parallels the C&O Canal on the south side and a steep, tree-covered hill on the north. It's here that traffic starts to pick up as you encounter commuters coming from the ritzy residences tucked away in the hills south of Bethesda, Northern Virginia commuters from McLean crossing Chain Bridge, or the many row houses around Georgetown University.

Canal Road ends just downhill from the Georgetown stadium, and becomes M Street, a narrow artery with trendy shops and restaurants on both sides, and cars and trucks jockeying for position to enter the city via M Street, cross Francis Scott Key Bridge into Rosslyn, or get on the Whitehurst Freeway to get into the city center, Foggy Bottom, or the many other federal buildings in Northwest DC.

I normally get off Whitehurst just pass Washington Harbor onto Rock Creek and Potomac Parkway, which takes me past the Kennedy Center for the Performing Arts , under the Theodore Roosevelt Bridge and around the west side of the Lincoln Memorial. There's a point where, for a few seconds, you can see the top of the memorial with the top of the obelisk that is the Washington Monument seem to grow out of the top of the memorial to our sixteenth president to your left, while off to the right the stark white gravestones of Arlington National Cemetery rise up toward the sky. After over a decade, it was a sight that still gave me goose bumps.

After circling the memorial, I got onto Independence Avenue at the north end of Potomac Park, drove past the Tidal Basin – most famous for a 1974 incident involving Senator Wilbur Mills and a stripper who decided to go skinny dipping in it during the early hours of the morning. I like it in the spring when the cherry trees that line it are in full bloom. During July, it's just a nice looking lake. Near the Bureau of Engraving, I turn onto Maine Avenue, and when I cross Fourteenth Street, the sightseeing ends. Efforts have been made to spruce up the area, but with the fish market and acres of low income housing, it still has a slightly industrial, working class appearance. Maine Street turns into M Street, and at the Waterfront Metro Station, I turn south on Fourth Street for the three block drive to my office. The Metro station is in a dingy shopping center containing a large food market, a drug store, and a few other stores that form an L from M Street to Sixth Street. It's just a few blocks north of my office, so I often leave the car parked and walk up to use the subway to get around town.

At half past noon, the parking lot in front of the building was full except for two of the three slots assigned to A. E. Pennyback, Confidential Enquiries.

Heather's little blue Honda was in its usual place, and I pulled in next to her. Our visitor slot was seldom used. There was an unwritten code among the building occupants; no one poached someone else's parking space. Of course, of the five other tenants, two accounting outfits, a watch repair shop, a tax preparer, and an astrologer, only the astrologer had a steady stream of customers, but most of them came on foot, so it really wasn't a problem. Heather and I were in the center unit on the second floor, between one of the accountants and the tax preparer. We don't get much foot traffic on the second floor.

She was at her desk, staring at her computer screen and making notes on a steno pad when I walked in.

"Hey, kid, what's up?" I started to walk past her desk.

"Hang on there, boss man," she said, holding up her steno pad. "I got something for you."

"You looked busy. I didn't want to disturb you."

"I'm always busy," she said, laughing. "I'm busy even when I'm not. When I have information for you, it's not disturbing me for you to hang about."

"Yeah, okay – I have no idea what that means. What do you have for me?"

I pulled the chair next to her desk around and straddled it. She took her time, slowly picking up the pad, taking a last look at the computer screen, nodding at something on it which, while it might have meant something to her, was just a mass of numbers and lines to me.

She swiveled her chair around and flipped her pad to the first page, and smiled at me. "Well now, let's start with Ms. Megan Sutliff," she said. "You want the complete bio, or just the juicy parts?"

I'd no doubt she'd managed to unearth more information about Megan than she probably remembered about herself, but I just wanted information that might pertain to why someone might want her dead.

"Let's stick to the juicy stuff," I said.

"Okay. That leaves out her childhood. Not much there anyway – just one private tutor after another. Things got interesting, though, when she went off to college. Do you know she could have gotten into any Ivy League school she wanted? Not just because her old man was as rich as Croesus, but because she aced her SATs – but, she went to some little back water college in West Virginia, Baldwin College. Got her B.S. in business administration and followed that up with an M.S. in psychology."

"So, she couldn't make up her mind what she wanted to do with her life," I said. "What's juicy about that?"

She put the pad on the desk and glared at me. "Would you please let me tell this in my own way?"

I held my hands up in surrender. "Okay, okay. Go ahead; just don't keep me hanging in suspense for the rest of the day."

"She wasn't such a great student at first," she said, picking up the pad. "Barely got passing grades in her courses, and missed a lot of classes. One of her professors talked her into entering therapy about midway through her freshman year, and she did a complete turnaround. She moved off campus to a small house in the area, buckled down, and finished the rest of her under-grad study with all A's."

"What was her problem?" I knew, but I was curious – had Heather been able to uncover information online that should be absolutely protected?

"I couldn't find out. All I was able to learn was that she was in therapy – for three years, in fact." Her brows furrowed and she looked askance at me. "Do you know why she was in therapy?"

It was tempting to leave her in suspense. But, Heather and I have worked together since I became a PI, and she is also on that short list of people I call friend. Besides, I know she'd never withhold information from me. I told her what I'd learned about Megan's relationship with her father. Her cheeks flamed red as I spoke.

"Oh, my goodness," she said. "That's horrible. I hope that old man burns in hell. It does explain, though, why she never went back home, not even during school vacations. She didn't return until after getting her graduate degree, and then she only stayed a few years. She left again for good – I guess that's when she went to North Carolina. She completely dropped off the grid ten years ago."

"By dropped off the grid, you mean there's *nothing* in the record about her?"

"Nothing that I can find. It's like she ceased to exist."

In a way, I thought, she did cease to exist. After her childhood, even with therapy, she would have been carrying around some powerful demons. I could play arm chair psychologist and guess that her therapy had helped her come to terms to a degree with what her father had done, but she needed to face him in order to be completely cured of her demons. Somehow, though, that hadn't worked, and she'd run away. Maybe her condition was the kind you never recover from. Whatever, it didn't really tell me who would want to kill her. If the old man had still been alive, I would have been tempted to suspect him. After all, if something like that became public knowledge, it would ruin him. He was dead, though – beyond the reach of public condemnation.

"Yeah, but I fear her past is coming back, not to haunt her, but to kill her," I said. "Unfortunately, as juicy as it is none of this information tells me who wants her dead. You got anything else?"

"On her, no, but I did find a few juicy tidbits about her twin brother, Melvin. He's quite the character – not at all like Megan."

"How can that be? Aren't twins supposed to share a lot of characteristics?"

"According to everything I've ever read, they do," she said. "But, if the information I found is valid, Megan and Melvin only shared common parents. She was always the serious one – except for the first few months of her freshman year in college, an outstanding student – while he barely scraped by academically. As teens, she studied, he played. In college, after therapy, she was an ace student. He got into Yale on the strength of his father's wealth and alumnus status, and squeaked through his under graduate studies with a weak 'C' average. He got just high enough score on his GRE to get in to graduate school and got his MBA, but again, just barely."

"This is the guy who is now running the company? No wonder she wanted to come back."

Heather beamed. She was always happy when I showed an interest in the nuggets she dug up.

"It gets juicier. When he came back from college, he lived the life of a rich playboy for a few years until Megan cut the family ties and disappeared. The old man took him into the firm as a junior executive, and about six months after Megan's departure, promoted him to vice president. For the past six years, he's effectively been Sutliff Pharmaceutical's chief executive officer, and that's when the real interesting stuff starts."

I looked at her, my left eyebrow arched. "Interesting? In what way is it interesting?"

"When the old man started getting sick, not too long after Megan left actually, Melvin took over the active running of the company. Rumor is, he began ordering short cuts to rush drugs to market – like shading test results, or outright faking them – he fired a lot of the senior management and brought in complete outsiders unfamiliar with the industry. There've been rumors, unproven but persistent, that he's also been siphoning cash from the company coffers and stashing it in an account in the Cayman Islands."

"Sounds like Melvin's been a bad boy," I said. "I'm surprised he hasn't been investigated by the feds."

"Well, since the company's privately owned and he and his sister are the primary stockholders now that the old man's dead, the Securities and Exchange Commission isn't really interested. The Food and Drug Administration has been looking at the rumors of him monkeying with drug tests, but they haven't been able to find any proof, so that's up in the air."

"Wouldn't someone be interested in his offshore bank account?"

"The IRS would, if they could prove it, but our boy's covered his tracks well. He might have been only a so-so student, but he's an ace at covering up his wrongdoing."

It would take someone who could get inside his mind to get a lead on what he was up to, and as I thought that, an idea exploded inside my mind like a bottle rocket on the Fourth of July. "Holy shit, Honeybunch," I said. "I think I know who wants Megan Sutliff dead."

Great minds think alike. The way her eyes went wide said she'd come to the same conclusion.

"Oh, that's just horrible," she said. "That family is really crackers."

Charles Ray

21.

Our assumption was further validated very shortly afterwards by a call from Corporal Toby Wells of the Dare County North Carolina Sheriff's Department.

"Al, Toby Wells here," he practically yelled into the phone. "We picked up some more information about Augie Small, and I thought you might find it of interest."

"Okay, Toby, but you don't have to yell in my ear. The connection's just fine. What do you have?"

He brought his voice down a few decibels. "Sorry. Down here, the phone system's hinky for days after a big storm, so you just get into the habit of speaking louder. Anyway, when we pulled Small's pickup apart, we found a small duffel hidden in one of the side panels that had twenty grand in it. The guy was a real pack rat – kept everything apparently. There was paperwork in the bag with the money, showing it had been wired to him at his address in Virginia from a bank in the Cayman Islands."

The connection wasn't concrete, but I don't believe

in coincidences.

"Did the paperwork show the account number?"

"It didn't show the complete number, just the last three digits," he said. "They were 555. I don't know if you can use that to track the account holder, but it's a lead anyway."

I repeated the numbers as he recited them, signaling Heather to start working her magic and see if she could trace the owner from just three digits. She frowned, but started pecking at her keyboard anyway.

"Not sure, Toby," I said. "But, it's worth a shot." If Heather couldn't track it, I was willing to bet the IRS could. It might take longer, and there was no guarantee they'd share what they found with me, but it was worth a shot. "Thanks, my friend. Let me know if anything else turns up."

I broke the connection.

"I don't think I'll be able to find out who owns this account even if we had the full number," Heather said. "The Cayman Islands have banking privacy laws that rival the Swiss. They've had a treaty with the U.S. for the past ten years or so, which allows them to share account information when there is an investigation of criminal activity, but that doesn't include nonpayment of income taxes. There's no way they'll release the information to a private citizen."

"Damn," I said. "And, they're unlikely to release it to even the IRS. Hey, you said the FDA's been looking into Melvin Sutliff's affairs – you think they might be interested in whether or not he has a bank account offshore?"

There, I'd put a name on the elephant in the room. The one person who stood to lose the most by Megan's presence in Washington, and therefore, the one most likely to benefit from her death, was her brother. With her out of the picture, he'd inherit the whole thing, but more importantly, she wouldn't be around to expose his activity, which could put him away for a good long stretch.

Heather snapped her fingers and smiled. "I have contacts at both agencies," she said. "A couple of secretarial school classmates who are senior administrative assistants now, working for some pretty heavy hitters. Let me give them a call and see what we can do."

That didn't leave me much to do. I still had a couple of hours before I needed to head for Megan's place to start another boring night of guard duty. I then realized that I'd not been in my own office since coming back from Manteo – probably tells you how little I actually do there. Might as well, though, so I went in.

It hadn't changed. Still just two-thirds the size of the outer office, with the same scarred old executive desk and high-back black leather executive chair I'd gotten at a military surplus auction, the wooden chair sitting at the side for the rare visitor, a book case under the window to my left with a few phone books and other reference books, and a couple of hunting prints on the wall beside the door, flanking the signed photo of me with General Colin Powell when he was chairman of the Joint Chiefs of Staff and I was assigned to the Pentagon just before retiring from the army.

Every horizontal surface was coated with a fine layer of dust. Heather hadn't come in during my absence either. We have a cleaning service included in our lease, but they only come twice a month. My week away must have come between their visits. I fished around in the top drawer of my desk and found a couple of old brown napkins from burger orders that I'd not used, and brushed off the seat and armrests of the chair and the front half of my desk. I picked up the keyboard to my computer and blew on it, creating a horizontal geyser of fine dust. With a bonus we'd gotten on a big case, I'd let Heather talk me into upgrading our computers, so we now both had little thin screens, detached keyboards, and small processors, that took up far less space than the old ones and had – so Heather told me – much more computing power. She kept bugging me to pay to network them, so we could communicate directly with each other without having to send emails, but the price tag, somewhere in the neighborhood of five grand, seemed too much for the small convenience. Hell, I hardly ever used my computer for anything but checking email and playing computer chess, which I always lost.

Once I was satisfied the keyboard was as clean as it needed to be, I reached under the desk and turned the processor on. I watched the screen do its little multicolored show and listened to the whirring of the machine under my desk. For a device that was supposed to be so much faster than the old one, it took just as long to be fully functional. Finally, though, the screen, bright blue with a black, yellow, and orange logo in the center, stopped flickering. I grabbed the mouse which sat on a little square to the right of the keyboard and began pushing it around, watching a little white arrow dance across the screen. A gray bar across the bottom of the screen, with a lot of unintelligible – to me – symbols was my target. At the left was a little square with the word 'Start' in it. I centered the arrow over the 'S' and pressed the left front. A rectangle popped up containing more symbols, fortunately with labels. I moved the arrow up to a blue lower case 'e' with a halo and clicked on it. When the Internet window stabilized, I clicked on 'Favorites' and selected 'email,' which pulled up my mailbox. As I'd feared, it was crammed with junk, mostly offers for things I'd never consider buying, and a couple of emails from some guy in Nigeria with an unpronounceable name telling me I could get a big hunk of change if I'd just send him my bank account details.

I spent twenty minutes deleting, closed my email, and clicked on the chess game. For the next hour, I beat my head against a metaphorical wall as the computer trounced me game after game.

My head can go up against a brick wall only so many times before I get the message. I finally logged out of the chess game, made another check of my email and deleted a few more promotional emails, turned my computer off and let Heather know I was heading home. I called Sandra's mobile phone, only to discover that she was still at Megan's. The two women had spent the entire afternoon talking – and had even gone out to a nearby Safeway and to pick up a few fresh items for Megan's larder. I heard her talking in the background, and when I asked, Sandra said they were in the kitchen chatting as they put things away. After some more murmuring, Sandra blithely informed me that we were having dinner with Megan, so I should just run home, get whatever I needed for the evening and meet them there.

I told her about the call from Wells in North Carolina and our discovery that Melvin Sutliff might be the person who hired the goon who went after Megan.

"Should I tell her?" Sandra's voice was low – almost a whisper.

"Maybe you shouldn't," I said. "We have no proof yet. I'm pretty certain, but I don't have anything that would stand up in court."

"Okay, you'll hurry then, won't you?" Now, I heard worry in her voice.

"I don't think you have anything to worry about. I asked the groundskeeper, Fuentes, to stay there until I arrived. I doubt anyone'll try to get at her before dark."

Another one of my hunches, and one that I hoped was right.

"Hurry anyway," she said.

22.

It was almost 5:00 by the time I pulled into my front yard, but the sun was still high above the tops of the trees in the forest behind the house.

I got out, locked the car, and went inside.

Funny how you can get used to things, I thought as I entered the empty house. For many years after my wife and son died I lived alone, and became accustomed to it – even preferred it. Then, I met Sandra, and after a fitful start to our relationship, she moved in with me, at first just staying a few days a week and returning to her little frame house in Takoma Park, but finally moving her stuff in and renting her house, making our living arrangement more or less permanent. Now, whenever she wasn't there, I felt her absence.

I stood in the center of the living room for a long time breathing deeply. The fragrance of her shampoo hung lightly in the air like a bouquet of lilacs.

Shaking myself out of my reverie, I went to the bedroom, to the closet where I keep my gear. I took a black jumpsuit, the one with extra pockets in sleeves and legs and loops at the waist and ankles, a black skull cap, and my black canvas-side boots out, putting the clothing on the bed. I stripped down to my underwear and began dressing, pulling on a pair of black stretch socks from a drawer, and then the jumpsuit. From the back of the closet shelf, I took down my K-bar knife in the black leather sheath and hooked it into the left ankle loop. I then sat on the edge of the bed and slipped my feet into the boots; lacing them up tightly – not so tight it cut off circulation, but tight enough so they wouldn't flop around and impede my movement. I tucked the skull cap into one of the leg pockets. Wouldn't do to have some motorist reporting seeing a man wearing a skull cap with eye holes down River Road.

The whole process took me thirty minutes. By 5:35 I was gunning the engine of the Volkswagen, heading toward River Road.

23.

I pulled the Volkswagen in behind Fuentes' pickup, parked in front of the garage, at 6:20. He was kneeling at a flower bed between the garage and the house, spreading mulch around the flowers. When he heard my car's engine, he stood and turned, wiping his hands on his pants and smiling at me.

"*Jola, Senor Al*," he said. "The two senoritas are waiting for you in the kitchen."

"Thanks, Miguel. You can go home now. I've got it."

"*Si, senor*, as soon as I finish mulching these plants."

He went back to his mulching. I walked to the kitchen and rapped lightly on the door.

Megan, clad in a pink blouse and blue skirt, over which she wore a red and white checked apron, opened the door. "Al, you're just in time, we just finished cooking supper." She stepped aside. "Come on in. Sandra's setting the table."

Her eyes became little round circles when she got a

closer look at me, especially the wicked looking knife strapped to my ankle.

"Just in case," I said.

Sandra came into the kitchen. She smiled when she saw me. She came over and gave me a hug and a peck on the cheek. She took in the outfit.

"Table's all set, Megan," she said. "Are you ready to put the food out?" She then put her lips close to my ear and in a whispered voice asked, "You expecting trouble tonight?"

I shook my head. "Just being prepared," I whispered back.

Megan stood near the tabletop counter installed in the center of the kitchen holding a large platter of breaded pork chops. She looked at us with a raised brow, skeptical expression. "Sandra, would you get the salad," she said. "And, then we can get the drinks and supper will be ready."

She walked past us, still with that skeptical look on her face.

"You're holding something back," Sandra said as soon as she was out of the room. "You *are* expecting trouble."

"No, honestly, I'm just being prepared," I said. "Look, I'll tell her everything I know after dinner."

Dinner was great. Breaded pork chops and stir-fried green beans with those little clover-leaf rolls and a garden salad with oil and vinegar dressing on the side. Sandra and Megan had white wine with theirs. I had to satisfy myself with iced tea. Even one beer would make me drowsy – not a good condition when you're supposed to be protecting someone's life.

After dinner, I helped them clear the table. Megan told us to leave the dishes in the sink to be done the next morning. We went into the living room, where they had more wine and I sat there nursing a cup of after dinner coffee; the first of many I'd drink to stay awake.

Megan held her glass up, letting the light from a lamp in the corner shine through the liquid. But, she wasn't looking at that, she stared at me around the side of the glass. "Okay, Al," she said. "Are you going to tell me what's going on?"

I put my glass on the table, leaned forward with my hands on my knees, and told her everything – what Heather had uncovered, what I suspected. She listened with an impassive expression on her face. When I'd finished talking, she took a sip of wine.

"I'm not surprised," she said. "I suspected Melvin sent that man to kill me the moment I saw the pickup drive up to the house. I didn't want to say anything, though, until you came to the same conclusion independently."

I had to admire how calmly she was taking the whole thing. Most people upon learning that a family member – or anyone for that matter – wanted them dead would be more than a little upset.

"It's really academic, but do you have any idea why your brother would want to kill you?"

"Two come to mind," she said. "First, I doubt that he wants to share management of the company with me. Especially since I'm far better at it and would displace him within weeks. Secondly, you mentioned the offshore bank account. I think he's been siphoning money from the company and depositing it there. Inside the company, I'd be able to prove it, and he knows it."

"That's pretty much the same conclusion I came to," I said. "At first, I wondered why he'd not come after you long ago, but I guess as long as your father was alive, he felt safe."

Her lips turned down in an angry snarl. "Yeah - he knew that as long as dad was alive, there's no way I'd ever have come back here."

"Well, he hired one hit man, so we have to assume he'll just look for another."

"And, another, and another," she said.

Sandra put a hand on her shoulder. "Don't worry, Megan," she said. "Al will find a solution to this. He always does."

If only it was that simple. I couldn't guard her forever. The real answer to her problem was to stop Melvin, but in order to do that I had to have proof that would stand up to legal scrutiny. If Heather could tie him to the Cayman's bank account, that might be enough, but it would be even better to tie him directly somehow to Small. As puzzles went, this one was like having a giant jigsaw puzzle that was mostly of a cloudless blue sky, with most of the corner pieces missing and no picture on the cover. I had a general idea, but no starting point. It was going to be another long night.

Charles Ray

24.

The three of us sat in the living room talking until nearly midnight. Megan had cleaned the guest bedroom for Sandra, who'd decided to spend the night. Before the two them retired to their rooms, I checked them out, making sure the windows were securely locked. I then checked the rest of the upstairs, and once I was satisfied that there was no way to access it except from the ground floor – unless the intruder was a bat – I bid them good night and went back downstairs.

I did a thorough inspection of the ground floor, paying particular attention to the kitchen. After making sure all the doors and windows were locked, I went back to the living room. I sat there on the sofa in the dark, a pot of coffee and a mug on the table at my knee. In a few minutes, my eyes had adjusted to the lack of light and I could see outlines of the furniture, the light rectangles marking the windows and doors both front and rear.

The sofa was comfortable, too comfortable actually. I poured a mug of coffee and took a sip, and then I got up and walked around the room, being careful not to go too near windows. I realized after the second circuit that my caution was wasted. My car was parked where it could be seen, and so was Sandra's. I had another night of sleeplessness and no activity to look forward to.

Tired of walking around, I sat back on the sofa. I must have dozed off, because I heard a ringing in the distance, which turned out to be my cell phone which I had in one of my sleeve pockets. I looked at my watch. It was half past one in the morning. I squinted at the display panel on the phone, not recognizing the number at first. Finally, the numbers resolved themselves – it was Heather.

"Heather," I said. "Why the hell are you calling me at such an ungodly hour?"

"Oh, sorry, I was sitting here on the computer and I guess I lost track of time."

"On the computer? Are you still in the office?"

I must introduce her to a man, or somehow get her a life, I thought.

"Yeah, I'm still here," she said. "My contact at Treasury had to make some calls and just got back to me a few minutes ago."

Not only did she need to get a life, but many in her circle of contacts did as well. "Okay, but as soon as you hang up, you get your tush home, you hear. And, don't you think about coming to work before noon tomorrow, I mean today."

"If you insist. Anyway, my Treasury contact said they were able to confirm that the account from which the money to Small was transferred belongs to one Melvin Sutliff. She wanted to know how we got it."

"I hope you didn't tell her . . . too much," I said.

"I had to give here something. These things work on a quid pro quo basis, you know. For every quid I get I have to give up a little quo. I told her we got it from a sheriff's office in North Carolina in connection with a home invasion that happened when you were down there. When she pressed for more, I told her that's all I knew."

It wouldn't take the feds long to figure out what was going on. They're not totally incompetent, just slow sometimes. But, Heather had bought us some time. Now, all I had to do was figure out how to tie Melvin to an attempt to kill his sister.

"Okay, honeybunch, you did good. Now, go home and get some sleep. See you this afternoon."

For the next five hours I thought about how I would be able to protect Megan without anyone knowing about it. How would I get into the house without being seen. Fuentes arrived at 6:30 with my answer.

Charles Ray

25.

After a brief conversation with the groundskeeper, Sandra and I went home. We did our four-mile run through the forest behind the house, worked out on the heavy bag in the barn for twenty minutes, and then, after showering together, did a light breakfast. I meditated for ten minutes after breakfast – I usually do twenty minutes, but Sandra had other exercises in mind – and then we both went to bed. After Sandra got out of bed, I fell asleep until noon.

I was awakened to the aroma of fresh-brewed coffee. I rolled out of bed, took a quick shower and put on a clean set of black coveralls, complete with all my gear from the previous evening. Sandra and I ate a quick lunch together, listening to the news report on NPR as we ate. The weather man came on at the end of the news with a forecast of inclement weather moving into the Washington area from the southwest – a storm front, with possible high winds, thunderstorms, and heavy rain.

After helping Sandra clean the kitchen, I drove by the office to check my emails. Heather had ignored my order to stay home, but she looked fresh, so I assumed she'd at least gone home and got a few winks. She hadn't, however, learned anything new. I briefed her quickly on my plans for the evening.

Don't ask me why I thought it would work. The years of secretive missions in even more secretive locations has given me a sixth sense about these things. Like animals can sense an impending storm, I sense when danger is coming, and my senses were tingling. I called Fuentes cell number and told him that I was on my way.

I drove to the big Home Depot store on Shady Grove Road just west of Maryland Route 355, and parked in the ground level covered lot in front of the store's main entrance. Miguel Fuentes was waiting for me in front as we'd agreed. When he saw me, he waved and pointed to his pickup truck that was parked two rows across me and closer to the exit. I joined him there.

"I apologize in advance, *senor*," he said. "But I had to buy four bags of manure in addition to the mulch."

He pulled back the canvas covering the bed, and the odor hit me like a punch to the face. The sweet and acrid smell of what's left after cows digest grass made my eyes water.

"Do you have a scarf or handkerchief that I can use? I didn't think to include that in my equipment," I said.

He pulled a large red bandana from his back pocket. "This will help *un poco*," he said. "Just don't breathe in too hard. The drive will only take a few minutes."

A few minutes under a canvas breathing cow shit would, I knew, feel like hours. But, I took the bandana, tied it over my mouth and nose, and hopped over the side of the truck bed. He pulled the canvas back into place, and after hearing the door slam and the coughing of the old engine catching, I felt the bumping as the vehicle pulled out of the parking structure and onto the street.

It did seem like hours – although a check of my watch showed it had only been twenty-five minutes – until the rattling old truck finally came to a stop and the engine was turned off. It was 3:30. When Fuentes pulled the canvas back, I almost knocked him over in my haste to get out of the truck. Taking the bandana off, I took deep breaths. It took me almost a minute to get the odor out of my nose, but I could swear I still tasted it. When I could finally breathe normally, I looked around. We were parked between the semi-detached garage and the kitchen. Someone would have to be inside the property and directly behind the house to see me, and the trees in that direction were widely spaced, so I considered it unlikely that I'd been spotted.

"*Gracias*, Miguel," I said. "I think you should follow your normal routine today. Leave when you normally would."

"Are you sure you do not need help, *senor?*"

He meant well. I imagine he'd do just about anything for Megan – more than I could say for her blood relations – but, I had enough on my hands trying to keep her alive. I didn't need an extra person to look out for. There was also the problem that if his truck was seen, it might scare an intruder off, and that's not what I was hoping for.

"Yeah, I think I can take care of it," I said. "But, thanks for the offer."

He smiled at me, but worry still clouded his expression. He turned away and began hefting the bags of manure and mulch from the truck. I took one last look around and then made my way to the kitchen door. I rapped lightly. Megan came into the kitchen. When she saw me, she looked surprised.

"Al, I wasn't expecting you until later this evening."

"I'm hoping you're not the only one," I said as I slipped inside the house.

26.

We spent the next three hours sitting in the kitchen, her fixing supper, and me sitting back from the window so that I could see into the backyard, but not be seen. The only sound was the thunk of a knife on the wooden chopping board as she diced lettuce and tomatoes for a salad. She'd offered to fix something more elaborate, but I convinced her that a light meal would be better. I needed to be alert, and a heavy meal might make me drowsy no matter how much coffee I drank.

At half past six, we sat at the little square kitchen table and had tossed salad with Thousand Island dressing and tuna on toasted rye bread, washed down with lemonade from freshly squeezed lemons. After supper, I made a pot of coffee while she cleared the table.

When she'd finished washing and rinsing the dishes, she looked at her watch. "It's only 7:15," she said. "Far too early to go to bed, so what do we do to pass the time?"

"I'll stay here in the kitchen. You do what you'd

normally do if you were here alone. Then, when you're ready for bed, turn off the lights down here and go upstairs."

Her brow furrowed. "I hate leaving you here all alone."

"Don't worry about it," I said. "I'm accustomed to spending time waiting quietly. I've had to sit for hours alone and in silence before."

Most people would have asked where and why I got such training, but she'd seen the outcome of my encounter of the intruder in North Carolina, so I think she had an idea. She didn't ask.

"Nevertheless, I think I'll just sit here with you for a while, if you don't mind. The fact is I really don't want to be alone right now."

I guess she'd been alone long enough – given what she'd told us about her father and her relationship with her twin brother, most of her life. I pulled a chair up to the table and straddled it, motioning for her to sit opposite me. "Sure," I said. "What do you want to talk about?"

She walked to the counter and filled two large mugs from the coffee pot. Returning to the table, she put one in front of me and took the chair facing me across the table.

"You know my sordid history," she said. "I'd like to know what makes Al Pennyback tick."

I took a sip of the hot liquid and put my mug down.

We talked – mostly, I talked – until a quarter to midnight. I told her things that I'd only told Sandra, not everything, mind you, but more than I usually share with anyone. She nodded at the appropriate times, and expressed shock at others, but otherwise kept quiet. When I'd run out of things to say, she took her mug to the sink, rinsed it out, and put it on the rack to dry. Then she turned out the kitchen light as I'd requested, and went into the dining room and living room, turning out the lights as she went.

I waited until I heard her footsteps on the stairs. My eyes had adjusted to the dim light of the Moon shining through the slits in the drapes over the windows. I walked into the living room and sat on the bottom step of the stairs.

There was nothing to do now but wait.

Charles Ray

27.

At around one in the morning, the wind outside picked up, making a mournful sound in the trees. I could hear the low rumble of thunder in the distance. I hoped the bad weather wouldn't spoil things. I was ready for this play to reach final curtain.

I sat there until 1:30, long enough that my calf muscles started to tighten up, but I didn't dare get up and move around. I stretched my legs out, lifting them up and down to loosen the muscles.

It was a long shot I was playing, but that little itch in my mind was going full blast. My gut told me it was near.

At first I didn't hear the sound. All I heard was the occasional boom of thunder seeming to come nearer, the creaking of the wood in the cool night air and the hum of the air conditioning system. But, then, there was a new sound. Just on the edge of my consciousness. A sound that didn't belong.

There was a 'snick' of metal brushing against metal from near the front of the living room, and then the door opened a crack. A dark figure slipped through the crack and the door closed. I eased to my right, hugging the wall. There was the scuffling sound of soft soled shoes on the carpet, and I could sense the figure moving closer.

From the stairs to the door it was a total of about thirty feet. The figure was about half the distance when I saw its right hand – held away from the body, I could see the unmistakable shape of a wicked looking automatic pistol. I couldn't see it clearly, but it had the short-barrel, blocky appearance of a SIG Sauer or a Beretta. Given who I thought the gunman was, my bet was it was the more expensive Beretta.

About ten feet from where I sat in a half crouch, ready to spring, the figure stopped.

The head tilted to the side, then up. There was a sniffing sound. I flattened myself further against the wall, sliding upright. I was pretty sure he couldn't see me against the dark wall – he'd just come in from outside, and his eyes hadn't had time to adjust from the Moonlit outside to the darker interior of the living room, the human eye doesn't adapt that fast to changed light levels. I'd showered with odorless soap, and I made sure my scouting gear was never washed in anything with a scent. I couldn't believe his senses were sharp enough to smell my normal human odor. Maybe it was just a warning from his lizard brain, that part of the mind we don't fully understand. The part that was essential to our prehistoric ancestors, but which in most modern humans is about as useful as an appendix or tonsils. We can get buzzes from it, but most people don't recognize them for what they are – warning signs that danger is near. The one time it does trigger a reaction, though, is when we're in a dark place. In the dark, the mind is already working overtime. Giving more significance to sounds, sights, and smells than they ordinarily warrant – sometimes.

We stood like that for a long time – at least a minute. Two still dark figures. Me waiting for him to make a move, and I assume, him trying to figure out what was spooking him. Well, that was fine with me. I had all night. I doubted he'd be able to stand there longer than a few more minutes before his muscles started seizing up. Not too many people are trained to remain still for very long. Even when they sleep, they move.

I was something else. In special operations, we'd been taught to stand, kneel, or lie absolutely still for hours. Ants crawling up your legs, and biting your scrotum, you ignore it. Flies crawling across your lips, you ignore it. When you're in an ambush position, or scouting an enemy location up close, the movement of an arm or leg, even swiveling the head, can give you away, blowing the mission – or getting you killed. I could, if I had to, stand there with my back against the wall all night. I could track the shadowy figure's movements with my eyes without moving my head, and I breathed slowly through my partly opened lips. Breathing through the nose, believe it or not, causes a slight sound that can be heard from three or four yards away by someone with acute hearing.

Just as I anticipated, after three minutes, one leg

and then the other twitched. I heard a low 'hnh' sound. His muscles had probably started to cramp up. That is painful.

He shook his right leg, and then his left. With the gun hand out in front, he started forward again. First, he veered to the right, peering into the corner where the sofa sat, and then he moved toward the door to the dining room.

As he moved closer to the dining room, he passed under the stairwell and out of my range of vision. I took that opportunity to ease down off the step onto the floor, still pressed against the wall.

A few seconds later, he came back into the living room, and started toward the end of the stairs.

I set myself, my muscles just tense enough to facilitate rapid movement. As he turned at the foot of the stairs, I could just make out vague details of his face – I recognized him from Quincy's office. His eyes widened – showing more clearly even in the dimness.

"Wha- " I jabbed at the eyes with my right hand, the first two fingers bent in a claw shape so that the second joints of the fingers made contact with his eyeballs. "Ow!"

As his head snapped back, I reached down with my left hand, grabbing his wrist in a vice-like grip and squeezing as I pushed it to the right.

His eyes clenched shut and his mouth formed an 'O.' He had just enough time before the pain in his wrist became too much to contract his finger and get off one shot. There was a flash in the dark, and the boom of the pistol echoed inside my skull. The ejected cartridge hit the stair rail and bounced off somewhere in the room. I squeezed harder and twisted my hand to the left. There was a snap, like a twig breaking, followed by a scream that hurt my ears.

The pistol fell from his fingers, making a dull sound as it landed on the stairs.

I pulled my right hand back and formed a fist. Then, I jabbed it forward. I felt the crunch of the bones in his nose fracturing under my fist.

Just then there was a flash of lightning, followed almost immediately by a boom of thunder. The room lit up. I could see that I'd won the fight.

The human body has a number of ways to react to pain. The first is to remove itself from the source of pain. Often, though, severe pain causes secretion of chemicals in the body that slows the heart beat and constricts the blood vessels, making it hard for the heart to pump blood to the brain. When this happens, the person faints.

Melvin Sutliff had suffered major pain – the shot to his eyes was probably not hurting as much, but it still had to sting – what with a broken wrist and now a broken nose. It was probably too much for his body to endure. In the seconds that the lightning had illuminated the room, I watched his eyes roll back in the sockets, his face slacken, and just as the room was plunged back into darkness, he slumped to the floor.

I started feeling along the wall for a light switch. There was another flash, and I reflexively tensed awaiting the sound of thunder which never came. After a couple of heartbeats, I looked up to see Megan Sutliff standing at the top of the stairs, her hand still on the light switch. She was looking from me to the crumpled body of her brother. I was looking from him, to her, to the black Beretta lying on the bottom step.

"Are you okay? I heard a shot," she said. She clasped her free hand over her mouth. "Oh, my God, you're bleeding."

Like I said, the human body has a number of ways to react to pain. One, of course, is to block it out. That's what I'd done. I hadn't even been aware of the bullet from the Beretta grazing my shoulder. It had torn a gouge out of the cloth of my coverall and plowed a little furrow into the fleshy part of my shoulder. It would leave a scar, but otherwise hadn't done any major damage. Flesh wounds, because of the damage to capillaries, tend to bleed a lot – less than if a vein or artery is struck, but enough to look gross – but not enough to be dangerous. As I looked at the damage to shirt and shoulder, my brain decided to acknowledge the signals from the nerve endings near the wound. It stung like bloody hell.

I clapped my right hand over it. "It's worse than it looks," I said through gritted teeth. "Just a flesh wound."

She looked down at her brother. "What about him?"

Except for the slow rise and fall of his chest, he

wasn't moving.

"He'll be out for a while," I said. "Fortunately for him, because when he wakes up he's gonna feel some major pain."

"Good," she said, without emotion.

"Now, I think you'd better call the police."

I turned with my back to the wall and slid down slowly on the bottom step.

Charles Ray

28.

The cops arrived in force within fifteen minutes. Megan's neighborhood is upper middle class and not too far from the residence of the U.S. vice president, so the police pay it attention.

The wind had died down and I could no longer hear thunder.

Two squad cars, a sedan with two plain clothes detectives, a crime scene van and an ambulance crowded the driveway. The medical technicians took a look at Melvin, putting an emergency splint on his wrist and a tape across the bridge of his nose to keep the broken bones from shifting. They then put him on a stretcher, with his good arm handcuffed to the side and, with a uniformed cop escorting them, took him out to the ambulance. Before leaving, the tech looked at my shoulder. He swabbed it with disinfectant and put a Band-Aid over it, warning me to be careful about showering, and to remember to change the dressing daily.

The two detectives took statements from Megan and me – me in the living room and her in the dining room. I told the guy who took my statement, a young black man with a military-style haircut and shoulders that threatened to burst out of his jacket, everything, including the incident in North Carolina – leaving out the information about Megan's father.

When he'd finished writing down what I said, he put his pen back in his pocket, closed his notebook and blew air through his cheeks. "Man, these rich dudes amaze me," he said. "Cat's coming into more money than he can spend in two lifetimes, and he don't want to share it with his own sister."

"For some people, all the money in the world is still not enough," I said. "In Sutliff's case, though, he was also afraid his sister would find out he'd been stealing from the company – he'd go to jail."

"Now, that is real dumb. Stealing from yourself. This dude's gonna be behind bars for a good long time. I will *never* understand rich people."

Makes two of us, I thought. The rich do seem to inhabit a different universe than the rest of us. Megan was something of an exception to that. Maybe all those years living *sub rosa* in North Carolina, having to get by on the proceeds from her trust fund had changed her. Unlike most of the rich people I'd encountered in my time, she seemed able to take a genuine interest in other people.

The other detective, a slightly older, but no less muscular white man with salt and pepper hair that was in need of a trim, had finished taking Megan's statement. The two detectives huddled near the front door, and after a while let us know they were leaving.

"We'll need the two of you to come to the precinct and sign typed versions of your statement," the white cop said, handing us his name card. "But, I think this is a pretty cut and dried case." He looked at me. "I can't believe you went unarmed against a guy with a Beretta and all you got was that scratch."

"Yeah," I said. "I moved a little slow on that. I think the thunder and lightning must have thrown my timing off."

"Huh?" His mouth gaped open.

"You don't know who this dude is, do you," his partner said. "This is none other than the Brown Knight."

The white cop's eyes narrowed, and then widened. "Oh, shit yeah," he said. "You're that PI that chick at the *Washington Post*'s always writing about."

"He's running buddies with Buster Mayweather."

"That so? Buster's a good cop, so if you're friends with him, you're okay in my book." He held out a hand. I grasped it firmly and shook.

After the cops and ambulance with their flashing red, white and orange lights were gone, Megan and I stood in the center of the living room. Given what had transpired, the room was in fairly good order. There was a fist-sized hole in the wall at the bottom of the stairs, with a slight spatter of my blood around it. The hole had originally been nickel-size, but the evidence tech had widened it digging the bullet out of the wall.

"Sorry about the damage to your wall," I said.

"I'm sorry about the damage to your arm," she said.

"I've had worse."

We both laughed.

It was three in the morning. She was no longer in danger, but she didn't want to be left alone. She couldn't get back to sleep, and I wasn't sleepy, so we sat there in the living room drinking coffee until the sun came up.

29.

Conrad Sutliff's will was finally probated on Friday that week. There was no formal hearing, but Quincy invited Sandra and me to come with him and Megan Sutliff to the court house. No mention was made of Melvin, still recuperating in the prison ward of DC General with an armed cop on his door around the clock, and he was on routine suicide watch.

I didn't think that was necessary. Melvin Sutliff didn't strike me as the type to harm himself – at least not in that way. He'd confessed to trying to have his sister killed, and when that failed, taking matters in his own hands. He'd also hired an expensive, high-powered lawyer to represent him – Quincy's firm having declined to do so. Quincy said he'd probably plea bargain and end up serving five or six years behind bars. Even justice is different for the rich. A poor kid from DC's southwest or northeast who'd broken into someone's house with a gun would probably be looking at a minimum of fifteen years behind bars.

Quincy and Megan arrived at the courthouse before us, and when we entered the small anteroom where they were required to wait, we caught them in the middle of an argument.

"- still think you should contest your brother being left in the will," Quincy was saying.

Megan's expression was stony. "No, I can't do that," she said.

Quincy turned to us. "Maybe you guys can talk some sense into her," he said. He looked exasperated.

"Some sense about what? She's impressed me as a pretty sensible person," I said.

"I think she should ask that her brother forfeit his share of the inheritance," he said. "After what he did, he really doesn't deserve to get a penny."

"Despite what he did . . . or tried to do," Megan said, her fists clenched. "He's still my brother. Father wanted him to have half, and after deducting the amount he stole, I think he should get it – when he gets out of prison."

"What's to keep him from trying to kill you again?" Quincy asked. "Al might not be around to protect you next time."

I turned to Megan. "He does have a point."

"I think I know Melvin better than either of you. He's greedy, but he's also a coward. He came after me before thinking I wouldn't know it was him. Now that he's been exposed, he'll be afraid to try because he knows I'll be waiting for him. Besides, once he's convicted, he won't be able to involve himself in the company's management, so he'll be dependent upon me for his livelihood."

She'd thought things through, and it made sense – sort of. She seemed pretty sure of herself.

"You're willing to forgive him for what he tried to do?" I asked.

"The one thing I learned all those years I was hiding in North Carolina was forgiveness. First, I had to learn to forgive myself. For a long time, I blamed myself for what happened to me. Thanks to therapy, I was able to get past that and eventually see things for what they were. I forgave myself – even though there was nothing to forgive. I've even forgiven my father for what he did to me. What Melvin tried to do was small potatoes compared to that."

Sandra walked to her and clasped her in her arms, holding her close and stroking her back. "I think what you're doing is marvelous," she said. "Not for Melvin, but for yourself. It takes a lot of strength to do what you're doing."

I looked at Quincy who was standing there looking confused. "Sorry, buddy, but I think I agree with the ladies."

He shrugged. "Okay, if that's the way you want it. I just hope you know what you're doing."

I was convinced she did.

Charles Ray

30.

It's said that the wheels of justice grind slowly. In Melvin Sutliff's case, they fairly flew around. Two weeks after his father's will was probated, his lawyer entered a plea bargain with the DA's office and he was sentenced to ten years for attempted murder and fraud – with a chance for parole after four years. I wasn't betting on him serving one day past that four year mark, but by that time, Megan would have firm control of Sutliff Pharmaceuticals, and he'd be an ex-con with a felony record who was lucky she was willing to provide him with an income.

The evening after the sentence was announced Sandra and I met Megan at Seoul Gardens, a Korean restaurant we often frequented on Little River Turnpike in Annandale, Virginia.

She arrived in the parking lot right behind us at around 7:15. It was cool for late July, and a slight breeze was blowing. I hadn't seen her since the probate court, and almost didn't recognize her. She'd let her hair grow out, and it was waving in the breeze. Her long garments had been replaced by a skirt that hugged her figure and ended just below the knees – it too waved each time a stray breeze blew. I noticed that she had nice legs. Along with the longer hair, she now wore makeup, easing the severity of her features.

Sandra embraced her, and they blew air kisses near each other's cheeks. I stuck out a hand to shake, but she leaned in and kissed me on the cheek.

"I like the new look," Sandra said.

Megan did a pirouette, causing her skirt to flare out and show a flash of thigh. "It's not what I wear to the office," she said. "But, I figured it would be appropriate for an evening out with my two best friends. What do you think, Al?"

Damn if she wasn't flirting with me, and with Sandra standing right there. I noticed an impish look on Sandra's face. I hate it when women gang up on me. The two of them had gotten to be good friends.

"You look sexy," I said. "If I wasn't already spoken for, I'd . . . well, I'll let your mind work on that."

Two spots of red appeared on her cheeks, then she and Sandra laughed.

"You were right, Sandra," she said. "He's never caught with his guard down."

"He's an operator all right," Sandra said, hooking her arm in mine. "And, wait until he orders a Korean meal for you."

That's what it was all about. Megan had never had Korean food before – not many Korean restaurants on Roanoke Island – in fact she'd not experienced much of the world, living as she had as a hermit to stay out of her family's sights. She was becoming a part of that world now, and we were her guides.

I felt the coolness of the evening breeze on my face. The sky was bright blue, with hardly a cloud to be seen. The aroma of beef being barbecued Korean style competed with the odor of gasoline fumes from the heavy traffic on Little River Turnpike.

Once we were inside, and being led to a table in the back corner we could no longer smell the gas fumes, but I missed the feel of the wind caressing my cheeks.

I'd spent a good part of my own life fearing the wind. But, I know that there's a duality to everything – the wind can blow deadly, but it also sweeps the bad away.

Charles Ray

Other books by this author

Fiction

Angel on His Shoulder
She's No Angel
Child of the Flame
Pip's Revenge
Wallace in Underland
Further Adventures of Wallace in Underland
The Last Gunfighters
The Culling
The White Dragons
In the Dragon's Lair
Dragon Slayer
Frontier Justice: Bass Reeves, Deputy U.S. Marshal
Dead Letter and Other Tales

Buffalo Soldier series

Buffalo Soldier: Trial by Fire
Buffalo Soldier: Homecoming
Buffalo Soldier: Incident at Cactus Junction
Buffalo Soldier: Peacekeepers
Buffalo Soldier: Renegade
Buffalo Soldier: Escort Duty
Buffalo Soldier: Yosemite
Buffalo Soldier: Battle at Dead Man's Gulch
Buffalo Soldier: Comanchero

Nonfiction

Things I Learned from My Grandmother About Leadership and Life

Taking Charge: Effective Leadership for the Twenty-first Century

Grab the Brass Ring

There's Always a Plan B

African Places: A Photographic Journey Through Zimbabwe and southern Africa

A Portrait of Africa

Books for children

The Yak and the Yeti
Samantha and the Bully

About the Author

Charles Ray has been writing fiction since his teens. He won a Sunday school magazine writing contest when he was thirteen, and having his byline on a short story published in a national publication forever hooked him on writing. During his time in the army (1962-1982) he often moonlighted as a newspaper or magazine journalist, and was the editorial cartoonist for the Spring Lake (NC) News, a weekly newspaper, during the 1970s. In addition to his writing, he was an artist/cartoonist and photographer for a number of publications, including Ebony, Eagle and Swan, and Essence, and had a monthly cartoon feature and did several covers for Buffalo, a now-defunct magazine that was dedicated to showcasing the contributions of African-Americans to the country's military history.

After retiring from the army, he joined the U.S. Foreign Service, and served as a diplomat in posts in Asia and Africa until his retirement in 2012. He has worked and traveled throughout the world (Antarctica is the only continent he hasn't visited), and now, as a full time writer, continues to globetrot looking for interesting things to write about, draw, or take pictures of.

A native of Texas, he now calls Maryland home.
For more on his writing and other projects, check one of the following Web sites:

http://www.wattpad.com/user/CharlesRay1
http://charlesaray.blogspot.com
http://charlieray45.wordpress.com

http://www.twitter.com/charlieray45
http://www.facebook.com/charlieray45
http://www.flickr.com/photos/charlesray45/
http://www.viewbug.com/member/charlesray
https://www.facebook.com/UhuruPressbooks

www.ingramcontent.com/pod-product-compliance
Lightning Source LLC
Chambersburg PA
CBHW060138130626
46556CB00006B/2398